300 Junior Novel
Anticipation Guides

300 Junior Novel Anticipation Guides

Nancy Polette

A Member of the Greenwood Publishing Group

Westport, Connecticut • London

Library of Congress Cataloging-in-Publication Data

Polette, Nancy.
    300 junior novel anticipation guides / Nancy Polette.
        p. cm.
    Includes index.
    ISBN 1–59158–422–1
    1. Young adult fiction, American—Problems, exercises, etc. 2. Teenagers—Books and reading—United
States. 3. Values in literature. 4. Teenagers in literature. 5. Young adult fiction—Problems, exercises, etc.
I. Title. II. Title: Three hundred junior novel anticipation guides.
PS374.Y57P65 2006
813'.6099283   2006010344

British Library Cataloguing in Publication Data is available.

Library of Congress Catalog Card Number: 2006010344
ISBN: 1–59158–422–1

First published in 2006

Libraries Unlimited, 88 Post Road West, Westport, CT 06881
A Member of the Greenwood Publishing Group, Inc.
www.lu.com

Printed in the United States of America

The paper used in this book complies with the
Permanent Paper Standard issued by the National
Information Standards Organization (Z39.48–1984).

10 9 8 7 6 5 4 3 2 1

CONTENTS

INTRODUCTION

Anticipation Guides

An anticipation guide is a series of 10 or more values statements directly related to the selection to be read. The readers bring their experience to the guide in marking AGREE or DISAGREE next to each statement. After the selection is read, the readers reexamine their initial responses to see if their thinking has changed as a result of the reading.

Three Ways to Use Anticipation Guides

1. The readers mark either AGREE or DISAGREE next to the values statements related to what is to be read. Following the reading of the text, the readers reexamine their initial responses to see if they would now respond differently.

2. When a novel has been chosen for group reading, the guide for that novel is presented to the group, one statement at a time. The group votes to AGREE or DISAGREE with each statement as it is read aloud. The total numbers of votes to AGREE and DISAGREE are recorded for each statement. Upon the completion of the novel, the process is repeated. The initial responses and the new responses should be compared, in order to see if there are any differences between the initial numbers of votes and the new numbers. Discussion may follow on ways in which the novel did or did not change the thinking of members of the group.

3. The guides may be used as an introduction to the novels. Readers may wish to browse through the 300 novel guides presented here, to find those that seem most interesting. The books should be available, so that the student who finds an interesting guide can obtain and read the book to which it refers.

ABEL'S ISLAND

by William Steig, Farrar, Straus & Giroux, 1976

Put a check on the line under AGREE if you agree with the statement. Put a check on the line under DISAGREE if you disagree with the statement.

AGREE   DISAGREE

_____   _____   1. Every person has hidden talents and skills of which he or she is unaware.

_____   _____   2. Often, many good things come from a bad situation.

_____   _____   3. It is hope that keeps dreams alive.

_____   _____   4. When you are old enough to be married there is nothing more to learn.

_____   _____   5. The best life is an easy life with everything you want.

_____   _____   6. Being all alone on an island would be terrifying.

_____   _____   7. Not having to work for a living would be an ideal situation.

_____   _____   8. Exploring a strange place would be an exciting adventure.

_____   _____   9. When a problem seems too big to solve, give up.

_____   _____   10. Sometimes you are your own worst enemy.

_____   _____   11. A frozen mind can lead to disaster.

_____   _____   12. Returning home after a year away, you would expect to find everything just as you left it.

ACROSS FIVE APRILS

by Irene Hunt, Follett, 1964

Put a check on the line under AGREE if you agree with the statement. Put a check on the line under DISAGREE if you disagree with the statement.

AGREE   DISAGREE

_______   _______   1. Young people are idealistic until they meet the real world.

_______   _______   2. In war, members of the same family have fought on opposite sides.

_______   _______   3. You can depend on the newspaper for accurate news.

_______   _______   4. One thought to be an enemy may turn out to be a friend.

_______   _______   5. A mob will commit terrible acts that an individual member of the mob would never commit alone.

_______   _______   6. Many young people have been forced by circumstances to assume adult responsibilities.

_______   _______   7. There is never any excuse for a soldier to desert his or her post in war.

_______   _______   8. Doing the right thing can sometimes get you into trouble.

_______   _______   9. If you defend a person everyone believes is in the wrong, you will tarnish your own reputation.

_______   _______   10. All actions have repercussions.

_______   _______   11. Sometimes in a situation there is no clear right and no clear wrong.

_______   _______   12. War may cause people to feel and act as if they are much older than they are.

AFTERNOON OF THE ELVES

by Janet Taylor Lisle, Orchard Books, 1989

Put a check on the line under AGREE if you agree with the statement. Put a check on the line under DISAGREE if you disagree with the statement.

AGREE   DISAGREE

_______   _______   1. Some people have eyes that seem to see everything.

_______   _______   2. A child with a reputation for stealing and lying would be a poor friend.

_______   _______   3. An elf village would appear in an overgrown backyard only in a fantasy tale.

_______   _______   4. Caring parents refuse to let their children associate with anyone with a bad reputation.

_______   _______   5. Having one good friend can make up for not having a family.

_______   _______   6. There may be a good reason why a mother neglects her children.

_______   _______   7. When life in the real world becomes intolerable, children often create imaginary worlds.

_______   _______   8. Stealing food is not wrong if children are hungry and there is nothing to feed them.

_______   _______   9. Social workers try to make life better for poor families.

_______   _______   10. Children who don't wear coats in the winter enjoy the cold.

_______   _______   11. Most things that appear to be magic have a logical explanation.

_______   _______   12. The most important trait in a friend is loyalty.

AL CAPONE DOES MY SHIRTS

by Gennifer Choldenko, Putnam's, 2002

Put a check on the line under AGREE if you agree with the statement. Put a check on the line under DISAGREE if you disagree with the statement.

AGREE   DISAGREE

_____   _____   1. No one would choose to live on Alcatraz Island.

_____   _____   2. An older brother should never be expected to take care of an autistic younger sister.

_____   _____   3. The best way to handle people who are different from you is to ignore them.

_____   _____   4. Children often perform some tasks better than adults.

_____   _____   5. Rules are made to be broken.

_____   _____   6. Don't start to put a plan into practice if you aren't sure whether it will work out.

_____   _____   7. When you know you are right, never back down.

_____   _____   8. Losing your temper for a good reason is okay.

_____   _____   9. Some parents won't take responsibility for their own children.

_____   _____   10. Some parents expect far too much from their children, expecting them to accept heavy responsibility before they are ready for it.

_____   _____   11. Sometimes bad decisions have good consequences.

_____   _____   12. You should not continue trying when a situation looks hopeless.

ALL THE WAY HOME

by Patricia Reilly Giff, Delacort, 2001

Put a check on the line under AGREE if you agree with the statement. Put a check on the line under DISAGREE if you disagree with the statement.

AGREE   DISAGREE

_______   _______   1. Some parents have no choice but to send their children to live with others.

_______   _______   2. Adults should not keep family secrets from teenage children.

_______   _______   3. Everyone wants a sense of belonging and a real home.

_______   _______   4. Running away is a poor way to solve a problem.

_______   _______   5. Having one good friend may make up for not having a family.

_______   _______   6. Everyone was poor during the Depression years.

_______   _______   7. There is nothing to fear but fear itself is a true statement.

_______   _______   8. A policeman can be a very good friend.

_______   _______   9. A journey of hope is the best journey to make.

_______   _______   10. A true friend will tell you your faults.

_______   _______   11. It is better to learn to live with a handicap than to pretend it does not exist.

_______   _______   12. Homesickness can be cured by keeping busy.

THE AMBER SPYGLASS

by *Philip Pullman*, Alfred A. Knopf, 2002

Put a check on the line under AGREE if you agree with the statement. Put a check on the line under DISAGREE if you disagree with the statement.

AGREE   DISAGREE

_____   _____   1. Everyone would like to have the power to seek the truth.

_____   _____   2. Mysterious creatures appear only in fantasy tales.

_____   _____   3. No scientist would experiment on human beings.

_____   _____   4. Some children are kidnapped for reasons other than money.

_____   _____   5. It is impossible to trust someone you fear.

_____   _____   6. It is possible to betray a friend without knowing it.

_____   _____   7. Some witches may be good, while some church members may be evil.

_____   _____   8. What a person does tells more about that person than what others say about him or her.

_____   _____   9. Parents would never do anything to cause their children harm.

_____   _____   10. Sometimes it takes a friend to help you keep up your courage in a difficult situation.

_____   _____   11. It is possible to fear and admire someone at the same time.

_____   _____   12. Love for another person can develop over a long period of time.

ANASTASIA KRUPNIK

by Lois Lowry, Houghton Mifflin, 1979

Put a check on the line under AGREE if you agree with the statement. Put a check on the line under DISAGREE if you disagree with the statement.

AGREE   DISAGREE

——————   ——————   1. Once you have a wart, it never goes away.

——————   ——————   2. Ten-year-olds can fall in love.

——————   ——————   3. It is no fun to visit old people.

——————   ——————   4. Baby brothers are bothersome and unnecessary.

——————   ——————   5. Marching to a different drummer is sometimes painful.

——————   ——————   6. Keeping lists is important, to prevent you from forgetting things.

——————   ——————   7. A new baby can disrupt an entire household.

——————   ——————   8. Laughing at someone is not always cruel.

——————   ——————   9. All old people are forgetful.

——————   ——————   10. A true friend will tell you your faults.

——————   ——————   11. It is important always to say what you think.

——————   ——————   12. Poor handwriting can get you into trouble.

...AND NOW MIGUEL

by Joseph Krumgold, Crowell, 1954

Put a check on the line under AGREE if you agree with the statement. Put a check on the line under DISAGREE if you disagree with the statement.

AGREE   DISAGREE

______   ______   1. Most people define themselves by the work they do.

______   ______   2. Poor families are always unhappy families.

______   ______   3. A job out in the open is far more satisfying than a job in a building.

______   ______   4. The oldest brother gets all the attention in a family.

______   ______   5. The middle child is most often ignored by other family members.

______   ______   6. Wishing for something hard enough will make it come true.

______   ______   7. Parents are always proud when children receive stars on their schoolwork.

______   ______   8. The cry of a newborn lamb is one of the most beautiful sounds one can hear.

______   ______   9. Most very old people are crabby and do not want to listen to what children have to say.

______   ______   10. Sometimes, prayers are answered in unexpected ways.

______   ______   11. A good deed should be its own reward.

______   ______   12. Human beings climb more than one kind of mountain during their lives.

ARTEMIS FOWL

by Eoin Colfer, Hyperion Books, 2001

Put a check on the line under AGREE if you agree with the statement. Put a check on the line under DISAGREE if you disagree with the statement.

AGREE   DISAGREE

______   ______   1. Fairies exist and it is possible to capture one.

______   ______   2. Only criminals have criminal minds.

______   ______   3. If your relatives were underworld figures and con artists, you would keep that fact a secret.

______   ______   4. The Internet is an open door to experiencing creatures that you do not believe exist.

______   ______   5. A book written in code reveals secrets you would not want to know.

______   ______   6. Digital cameras can be used for more than taking pictures of friends.

______   ______   7. To trick someone deliberately is always wrong.

______   ______   8. Mythology has no relevance to life today.

______   ______   9. A so-called sidekick always does what you tell him or her to do.

______   ______   10. Only a scoundel would make a promise with no intention of keeping it.

______   ______   11. An obsession with the Internet can be harmful.

______   ______   12. A lot of action makes any book a fast read.

ASHES OF ROSES

by Mary Jane Auch, Laurel Leaf Books, 2004

Put a check on the line under AGREE if you agree with the statement. Put a check on the line under DISAGREE if you disagree with the statement.

AGREE   DISAGREE

______   ______   1. Most immigrants who came to America in the 1800s found a better life.

______   ______   2. Any immigrant with trachoma was refused admission to the United States and was sent back to his or her country.

______   ______   3. In the 1800s, factory workers worked under terrible conditions and had no way to make them better.

______   ______   4. Sometimes parents must leave their children for very good reasons.

______   ______   5. The one thing immigrants coming to America have in common is fear.

______   ______   6. Good often comes out of tragedy.

______   ______   7. When defeat seems certain, it is foolish to go into battle.

______   ______   8. If you make new friends, your old friends will be jealous.

______   ______   9. Other people can never take the place of your real family.

______   ______   10. Often when you see something wrong, it is best to keep quiet.

______   ______   11. A strong belief usually leads to sacrifice on the part of the believer.

______   ______   12. There would be no labor unions today if factory workers in the 1800s had not suffered many abuses.

THE BAD BEGINNING: BOOK ONE

by *Lemony Snicket,* HarperCollins, 1999

Put a check on the line under AGREE if you agree with the statement. Put a check on the line under DISAGREE if you disagree with the statement.

AGREE   DISAGREE

_____   _____   1. Most people would like to live in a mansion with a huge library.

_____   _____   2. To recover from a terrible loss, one must keep busy.

_____   _____   3. To keep a friend, you must constantly telephone him or her.

_____   _____   4. Only people who don't care about appearances live in a house that looks like a pigsty.

_____   _____   5. First impressions may be wrong.

_____   _____   6. A kindness does not have to be repaid.

_____   _____   7. When adults won't help solve a problem, children must act on their own.

_____   _____   8. Standoffish people are usually shy.

_____   _____   9. Without books, life would be dull.

_____   _____   10. It is not necessary to read a document before signing it, if a person you trust asks you to sign it.

_____   _____   11. A story without a villain would be a boring story.

_____   _____   12. No one wants to read a book with an unhappy ending.

BEARSTONE

by Will Hobbs, Macmillan, 1989

Put a check on the line under AGREE if you agree with the statement. Put a check on the line under DISAGREE if you disagree with the statement.

AGREE   DISAGREE

_____   _____   1. Running away from trouble will not make the trouble go away.

_____   _____   2. If you are forced to live with a stranger, you don't have to try to get along.

_____   _____   3. Believing in a lucky omen may change your life.

_____   _____   4. It is best to be silent if you don't agree with another's viewpoint.

_____   _____   5. A house and a home are the same thing.

_____   _____   6. Gentle words work best when someone is upset.

_____   _____   7. An example of displaced anger is hitting a wall instead of hitting a person.

_____   _____   8. If you do not reach a self-determined goal, set a different goal for yourself.

_____   _____   9. Revenge may be bitter rather than satisfying.

_____   _____   10. Remorse is a feeling that you experience when you have harmed someone else.

_____   _____   11. The best way to right a wrong is to say you're sorry.

_____   _____   12. Having an obsession may be either a good or a bad thing.

BECAUSE OF WINN DIXIE

by Kate DiCamillo, Candlewick, 2000

Put a check on the line under AGREE if you agree with the statement. Put a check on the line under DISAGREE if you disagree with the statement.

AGREE   DISAGREE

______   ______   1. Making new friends can be difficult if you don't have the right clothes.

______   ______   2. Children with one parent are better behaved than children with two parents.

______   ______   3. Preachers' children never get into trouble.

______   ______   4. Stray dogs are dangerous and should always be avoided.

______   ______   5. Children don't want to hear adults share memories of earlier times.

______   ______   6. First impressions of people are often wrong.

______   ______   7. Wanting something you can't afford is foolish.

______   ______   8. Loneliness can be cured by keeping busy.

______   ______   9. You should avoid anyone who has served time in prison.

______   ______   10. People who have set routines are afraid to try anything new.

______   ______   11. Some people are more interesting than others because they have lived longer.

______   ______   12. You should see with your heart rather than your eyes.

BECOMING NAOMI LEON

by Pam Munoz Ryan, Scholastic, 2004

Put a check on the line under AGREE if you agree with the statement. Put a check on the line under DISAGREE if you disagree with the statement.

AGREE   DISAGREE

_____   _____   1. It is easy to love a little brother, even if he is sometimes a pest.

_____   _____   2. Grandparents are too old to raise their grandchildren since they do not understand the younger generation.

_____   _____   3. Having a special talent is useless unless you work hard to develop it.

_____   _____   4. Only responsible people make lists of things to be done.

_____   _____   5. Some people abandon children for selfish reasons.

_____   _____   6. Only a loving mother would give her child to someone else to raise if she felt the child would benefit.

_____   _____   7. People with ulterior motives eventually give themselves away.

_____   _____   8. A physically handicapped child should be motivated, not pitied.

_____   _____   9. A physically handicapped child needs more love than a normal child.

_____   _____   10. Some people are so self-centered that they act only from selfish motives.

_____   _____   11. Worrying is a useless activity. It will not solve a problem.

_____   _____   12. You should see with your heart rather than your eyes.

BELLE PRATER'S BOY

by Ruth White, Farrar, Straus & Giroux, 1996

Put a check on the line under AGREE if you agree with the statement. Put a check on the line under DISAGREE if you disagree with the statement.

AGREE   DISAGREE

______   ______   1. Grandparents are too old to understand children today.

______   ______   2. Wit, gentleness, and loyalty are human traits and of the three, loyalty is the most important.

______   ______   3. Most children who grow up without their parents end up in trouble.

______   ______   4. Two people who lead very different lives are not likely to become friends.

______   ______   5. Good friends bring out the best in each other.

______   ______   6. An intolerable situation is one that cannot be changed.

______   ______   7. People are quick to judge others by their appearance.

______   ______   8. In order to be yourself you must upset others.

______   ______   9. Many people are natural storytellers and don't realize it.

______   ______   10. It is better to have one good friend than many acquaintances.

______   ______   11. Bad dreams at night reveal daytime fears.

______   ______   12. A wink is a powerful form of communication and requires a response.

BEN AND ME

by Robert Lawson, Little, Brown, 1939

Put a check on the line under AGREE if you agree with the statement. Put a check on the line under DISAGREE if you disagree with the statement.

AGREE   DISAGREE

_______   _______   1. It is wrong to take credit for another person's ideas.

_______   _______   2. When a bargain is made, every effort should be made to keep it.

_______   _______   3. A proverb is a wise saying that should be heeded.

_______   _______   4. Incorrect information can cause a lot of problems.

_______   _______   5. Calm observation is important when lightning strikes.

_______   _______   6. A rift in a friendship may be due to a misunderstanding.

_______   _______   7. Discipline in an army is absolutely essential.

_______   _______   8. Inventors see ordinary objects in new ways.

_______   _______   9. It is possible to combine fact and fantasy in the same story.

_______   _______   10. A good deed may sometimes cause problems for other people.

_______   _______   11. A hero is a person who performs a brave deed without fear.

_______   _______   12. A mouse can communicate with a person only in a fantasy tale.

THE BFG

by *Roald Dahl*, Farrar, Straus & Giroux, 1982

Put a check on the line under AGREE if you agree with the statement. Put a check on the line under DISAGREE if you disagree with the statement.

AGREE   DISAGREE

_______   _______   1. It is okay for writers to make up words that do not exist.

_______   _______   2. Looking out of a window late at night, you may see things you don't want to see.

_______   _______   3. People don't believe giants exist, because they read about giants only in fairy tales and fantasy stories.

_______   _______   4. Every child needs a good hiding place.

_______   _______   5. The best way to catch a dream is in a bottle.

_______   _______   6. Music is a universal language.

_______   _______   7. Breaking into someone else's home is always wrong.

_______   _______   8. Kidnapping someone to keep him or her from telling a secret is cruel.

_______   _______   9. The best way to keep from being seen is to hide in plain sight.

_______   _______   10. If a country is under attack, a single person cannot make a difference.

_______   _______   11. If someone is hard to understand, ask that person to repeat himself or herself.

_______   _______   12. Sneaking by palace guards to see a queen may get you into a lot of trouble.

THE BIG LIE

by Isabella Leitner, Scholastic, 1992

Put a check on the line under AGREE if you agree with the statement. Put a check on the line under DISAGREE if you disagree with the statement.

AGREE   DISAGREE

_______   _______   1. You should never believe rumors even when they are alarming.

_______   _______   2. Life in a town may change quickly if the town is occupied by an enemy.

_______   _______   3. A law that requires you to wear a symbol of your religion on your clothing is wrong.

_______   _______   4. It is permissible to have laws that favor one group of people.

_______   _______   5. There may be good reasons not to celebrate a birthday.

_______   _______   6. It would be impossible to make a two-day journey without food or water.

_______   _______   7. Even the worst food tastes good when you are really hungry.

_______   _______   8. Enemy soldiers are always careful not to injure innocent civilians.

_______   _______   9. A reunion with loved ones you have not seen for a long time may be both happy and sad.

_______   _______   10. Many families separated by war never find each other again.

_______   _______   11. People who are ill should not be expected to work.

_______   _______   12. The Holocaust was a terrible page in the history of the world.

THE BIRCHBARK HOUSE

by Louise Erdrich, Hyperion Books, 1999

Put a check on the line under AGREE if you agree with the statement. Put a check on the line under DISAGREE if you disagree with the statement.

AGREE   DISAGREE

_____   _____   1. Most people don't realize the important role that weather plays in their lives.

_____   _____   2. No one would want to change houses twice every year.

_____   _____   3. Little brothers are a pain and a bother no matter where they are found.

_____   _____   4. It is impossible to do business with those for whom you have no respect.

_____   _____   5. Wild animals have every right to share the Earth with humans and should never be destroyed.

_____   _____   6. An entire town or village may be destroyed by disease.

_____   _____   7. Everyone must do chores that he or she detests, so it is best to do them with a smile.

_____   _____   8. It is natural to be envious of an older brother or sister.

_____   _____   9. It is possible to fear and love someone at the same time.

_____   _____   10. Native Americans had a far greater respect for the land than did the non-Native American settlers.

_____   _____   11. If you meet a bear in the woods, the best thing to do is to stand very still.

_____   _____   12. Children look at their parents as role models and want to grow up to be like them.

THE BLACK PEARL

by Scott O'Dell, Houghton Mifflin, 1967

Put a check on the line under AGREE if you agree with the statement. Put a check on the line under DISAGREE if you disagree with the statement.

AGREE   DISAGREE

_______   _______   1. Sea monsters are found only in stories.

_______   _______   2. Pearl diving is a very dangerous occupation.

_______   _______   3. Braggarts often lie about themselves because they have low self-esteem.

_______   _______   4. Confronting your greatest fear is not as difficult as you think.

_______   _______   5. It is better to give away a valuable object than to sell it.

_______   _______   6. The right to take nature's sea treasures belongs to everyone.

_______   _______   7. It is okay to steal back something you have given away.

_______   _______   8. The stories that frighten children do not frighten adults.

_______   _______   9. Old fishermen's tales should never be believed.

_______   _______   10. Superstitious people are poorly educated people.

_______   _______   11. A good captain may make a bad decision if his ship is in danger.

_______   _______   12. A sea creature can be both beautiful and evil.

BLOSSOM CULP AND THE SLEEP OF DEATH

by Richard Peck, Delacorte, 1986

Put a check on the line under AGREE if you agree with the statement. Put a check on the line under DISAGREE if you disagree with the statement.

AGREE   DISAGREE

______   ______   1. Some teachers can make the most exciting literature boring.

______   ______   2. Closed clubs should not be allowed in high school.

______   ______   3. Every class has at least one student who is an outcast.

______   ______   4. Some people today have extrasensory powers that others do not possess.

______   ______   5. Small students are often unjustly picked on or bullied by their larger classmates.

______   ______   6. Practical jokes are never justified.

______   ______   7. A mandate from a ghost could happen only in a story.

______   ______   8. Many Egyptian tombs were plundered before their artifacts could be preserved.

______   ______   9. A shared task may bring people closer together.

______   ______   10. People who put down those less fortunate than themselves are basically insecure.

______   ______   11. Regardless of what others think, it is essential to be true to oneself.

______   ______   12. Before television was introduced, children had no way to entertain themselves in the evening.

THE BOGGART

by Susan Cooper, Margaret K. McElderry Books, 1993

Put a check on the line under AGREE if you agree with the statement. Put a check on the line under DISAGREE if you disagree with the statement.

AGREE   DISAGREE

_____   _____   1. Destroying a valuable object is an example of outrageous behavior.

_____   _____   2. Being nice to paying customers is not always easy.

_____   _____   3. Communicating in another land may be difficult even if you speak the same language.

_____   _____   4. Boggarts do not exist and have never existed.

_____   _____   5. Parents approve of those of their children's friends who are most like their own children.

_____   _____   6. Animals sense sights, sounds, and smells before humans do.

_____   _____   7. Good deeds may be misunderstood.

_____   _____   8. There is a difference between mischief and causing harm.

_____   _____   9. Strange events don't always have a logical explanation.

_____   _____   10. Homesickness can be cured by keeping busy.

_____   _____   11. Waking up with a sense of dread means you have had a bad dream.

_____   _____   12. Reporters are always on the lookout for unusual news.

THE BOOK OF THREE

by Lloyd Alexander, Holt, Rinehart & Winston, 1964

Put a check on the line under AGREE if you agree with the statement. Put a check on the line under DISAGREE if you disagree with the statement.

AGREE   DISAGREE

_____   _____   1. Heroes think more about others than they do about themselves.

_____   _____   2. In life, as in books, good always triumphs over evil.

_____   _____   3. Even the most menial of jobs can lead to a successful life.

_____   _____   4. A sword and a horseshoe have many things in common.

_____   _____   5. The only number that is used in a fairy tale or fantasy is three.

_____   _____   6. Sometimes it pays not to be practical.

_____   _____   7. Most people can become "glorious heroes" if the situation calls for heroism.

_____   _____   8. It takes some people a very long time to discover who they really are.

_____   _____   9. People have no control over their own destiny.

_____   _____   10. Evil is often cloaked in beauty.

_____   _____   11. One does not have to have royal relatives to have royal blood.

_____   _____   12. Every human being must have a purpose in life, for life to be meaningful.

THE BORROWERS

by Mary Norton, Harcourt, Brace, 1953

Put a check on the line under AGREE if you agree with the statement. Put a check on the line under DISAGREE if you disagree with the statement.

AGREE   DISAGREE

_____   _____   1. Borrowing items without their owner's knowledge is the same as stealing.

_____   _____   2. Living in a world without sunlight would be extremely depressing.

_____   _____   3. The more objects and items of furniture you add to a home, the more beautiful it will be.

_____   _____   4. Human beings often fear things they don't understand.

_____   _____   5. Every family has times when its members get along and times when they don't.

_____   _____   6. Children who are overly protected by their parents cannot grow into healthy adults.

_____   _____   7. Greed for material possessions may result in disaster.

_____   _____   8. Unexpected night-time visitors are never welcome.

_____   _____   9. Stories never really end; they can go on and on.

_____   _____   10. Children should be given freedom to explore, even if some harm might come to them.

_____   _____   11. Powerful human beings always take advantage of the weak.

_____   _____   12. Only a mentally unbalanced person would report to the police that dressed up mice were living under the kitchen floor.

THE BOXCAR CHILDREN

by Gertrude Chandler Warner, Albert Whitman, 1965

Put a check on the line under AGREE if you agree with the statement. Put a check on the line under DISAGREE if you disagree with the statement.

AGREE   DISAGREE

______   ______   1. You should never judge a person before you meet him or her.

______   ______   2. Running away from home causes more problems than it solves.

______   ______   3. Sleeping in the woods may be dangerous.

______   ______   4. You have to have money to eat every day.

______   ______   5. A dog can be a comfort when you are sad.

______   ______   6. To get a job, a very young person has to lie about his or her age.

______   ______   7. Children who hide and refuse to go to school may end up in prison.

______   ______   8. Children under 12 cannot survive without the help of adults.

______   ______   9. Sometimes it is necessary to reveal a secret you promised you would never tell.

______   ______   10. It would be impossible to live in a boxcar for a whole year.

______   ______   11. If you are asked to search for someone who does not want to be found, you should refuse.

______   ______   12. Something that starts out as an adventure may end up as a disaster.

THE BREAKER BOYS

by Pat Hughes, Farrar, Straus & Giroux, 2004

Put a check on the line under AGREE if you agree with the statement. Put a check on the line under DISAGREE if you disagree with the statement.

AGREE   DISAGREE

_____   _____   1. Some people have no friends because they choose to be loners.

_____   _____   2. Being expelled from school is one of the worst things that can happen to a young person.

_____   _____   3. Children from wealthy families are happier than children from middle-income families.

_____   _____   4. Children from totally different backgrounds can never be good friends.

_____   _____   5. Before child labor laws were passed in the United States, children under the age of 12 worked 12-hour days.

_____   _____   6. There are good reasons for not revealing who the members of your family are.

_____   _____   7. One should never defy a grandparent.

_____   _____   8. Unions are essential to the welfare of workers.

_____   _____   9. The best thing to do when torn between two courses of action is to run away.

_____   _____   10. Owners of mines and factories are concerned only with making money, not with the welfare of the workers.

_____   _____   11. Once a behavior problem, always a behavior problem.

_____   _____   12. Loyalty to family is more important than loyalty to friends.

BRIAN'S WINTER

by Gary Paulsen, Scholastic, 1996

Put a check on the line under AGREE if you agree with the statement. Put a check on the line under DISAGREE if you disagree with the statement.

AGREE   DISAGREE

_____   _____   1. The most important things to take on a camping trip are matches.

_____   _____   2. Walking alone in the wilderness can be comforting.

_____   _____   3. The cave dwellers left books in stone.

_____   _____   4. A campfire in a cave may be dangerous.

_____   _____   5. Wolf packs attack only sick animals.

_____   _____   6. The first snowfall of winter is something to be feared.

_____   _____   7. It is not possible for an individual in the wilderness to preserve food over a long period of time.

_____   _____   8. Wilderness areas are important to the Earth's overall surface.

_____   _____   9. One who has no contact with humans for months will forget how to speak.

_____   _____   10. It is possible to enjoy life with no books or television.

_____   _____   11. Every person has more courage and ability than he or she thinks.

_____   _____   12. Wilderness living can change a person's outlook on life.

BRIDGE TO TERABITHIA

by Katherine Paterson, Crowell, 1978

Put a check on the line under AGREE if you agree with the statement. Put a check on the line under DISAGREE if you disagree with the statement.

AGREE   DISAGREE

_______   _______   1. A boy should be embarrassed to be beaten in a race by a girl.

_______   _______   2. A boy and a girl can be best friends.

_______   _______   3. Sometimes it is difficult to talk to parents.

_______   _______   4. Sometimes children need a secret place to be alone.

_______   _______   5. It is possible to create magic in your head.

_______   _______   6. If you wish hard enough for something, you will get it.

_______   _______   7. New students are not always welcome in a class.

_______   _______   8. A true friend will tell you your faults.

_______   _______   9. When people are sad, silence can be helpful.

_______   _______   10. Self-pity is a luxury few people can afford.

_______   _______   11. Nothing can take away the pain of losing a loved one.

_______   _______   12. Most parents understand their children better than the children think they do.

THE BRONZE BOW

by Elizabeth George Speare, Houghton Mifflin, 1962

Put a check on the line under AGREE if you agree with the statement. Put a check on the line under DISAGREE if you disagree with the statement.

AGREE   DISAGREE

______   ______   1. Revenge seldom brings satisfaction.

______   ______   2. A cruel deed should be repaid with another cruel deed.

______   ______   3. There are good reasons for becoming a member of an outlaw band.

______   ______   4. It is possible to nurse hatred until it grows out of control.

______   ______   5. A bronze bow is a symbol for what no one can do.

______   ______   6. It is possible to come to accept and love your enemies.

______   ______   7. It is a wise person who is willing to accept help from others.

______   ______   8. People who sink into deep depression could feel happy if they wanted to.

______   ______   9. Sometimes, disobeying a parent is the right thing to do.

______   ______   10. To live a full life, everyone must have friends.

______   ______   11. It is possible to be a good friend to someone whose beliefs are very different from your own.

______   ______   12. It is not possible for human beings to change their basic beliefs.

BUD, NOT BUDDY

by Christopher Paul Curtis, Delacorte, 1999

Put a check on the line under AGREE if you agree with the statement. Put a check on the line under DISAGREE if you disagree with the statement.

AGREE   DISAGREE

______   ______   1. Moving from one foster home to another is bad for any child.

______   ______   2. When no one believes the truth, you should make up a lie.

______   ______   3. Every person needs rules for his or her life.

______   ______   4. It is best always to tell adults what they want to hear.

______   ______   5. Revenge is neither wise nor satisfying.

______   ______   6. When adults tell you not to worry, it is time to worry.

______   ______   7. When one door closes, another always opens.

______   ______   8. The truth can't hurt if no harm is intended.

______   ______   9. When high standards are set, most people will try harder.

______   ______   10. Perseverance is better than talent.

______   ______   11. You should never impose your dreams on someone else.

______   ______   12. Hitchhiking is very dangerous, and you should never do it.

BUNNICULA: A RABBIT TALE OF MYSTERY

by Deborah and James Howe, Atheneum, 1979

Put a check on the line under AGREE if you agree with the statement. Put a check on the line under DISAGREE if you disagree with the statement.

AGREE   DISAGREE

______   ______   1. At one time, vampires really existed.

______   ______   2. Wild animals make good pets.

______   ______   3. When two people want the same thing, the older one should get it.

______   ______   4. A vivid imagination may get a person into trouble.

______   ______   5. Staying up all night is fun.

______   ______   6. Late-night snacks may keep you awake.

______   ______   7. Parents often don't understand their children.

______   ______   8. A pet that does not behave should be punished.

______   ______   9. Jumping to conclusions often produces the wrong answer.

______   ______   10. With poor planning, things can go wrong.

______   ______   11. It is possible to send a message without words.

______   ______   12. Old pets often dislike new pets.

BY THE SHORES OF SILVER LAKE

by Laura Ingalls Wilder, Harper & Row, 1939

Put a check on the line under AGREE if you agree with the statement. Put a check on the line under DISAGREE if you disagree with the statement.

AGREE   DISAGREE

________   ________   1. A pioneer is one who explores new territory.

________   ________   2. Strangers were always welcomed in pioneer days.

________   ________   3. Pioneer life was harder on women than on men.

________   ________   4. A first train ride can be an exciting adventure.

________   ________   5. Having no neighbors means living a lonely life.

________   ________   6. Horse thieves were common in pioneer days.

________   ________   7. Wolves in the wilderness attack only at night.

________   ________   8. Free land goes to the pioneer who gets there first.

________   ________   9. When towns are built, wildlife disappears.

________   ________   10. Sleeping in a tent night after night is fun.

________   ________   11. Pioneers whose crops failed often went hungry.

________   ________   12. Pioneer life was dangerous and difficult.

CADDIE WOODLAWN

by Carol Ryrie Brink, Little, Brown, 1976

Put a check on the line under AGREE if you agree with the statement. Put a check on the line under DISAGREE if you disagree with the statement.

AGREE   DISAGREE

______   ______   1. In the 1860s, a pioneer girl was expected to be ladylike.

______   ______   2. Pioneer life was rugged and dangerous.

______   ______   3. The pioneers and the American Indians did not get along.

______   ______   4. It is okay to fight with a bully.

______   ______   5. Living on a farm means a lot of work for children.

______   ______   6. Going to school for only half the year would be great.

______   ______   7. Skating on a frozen pond can be dangerous.

______   ______   8. It is unwise to spread rumors.

______   ______   9. Pioneer neighbors often helped each other.

______   ______   10. Sometimes, being alone is a good thing.

______   ______   11. Rich people are happier than people with average incomes.

______   ______   12. Living up to parents' expectations isn't always easy.

CALEB'S STORY

by Patricia MacLachlan, HarperCollins, 1996

Put a check on the line under AGREE if you agree with the statement. Put a check on the line under DISAGREE if you disagree with the statement.

AGREE   DISAGREE

______   ______   1. The middle child of a family sees both sides of issues more clearly than the oldest or youngest child.

______   ______   2. It would be tough to have three sisters and no brothers.

______   ______   3. When family members don't speak to each other for years there must be a good reason.

______   ______   4. An illiterate person has a hard time functioning in today's world.

______   ______   5. Adults who have not learned to read are too old to be taught.

______   ______   6. A diary is a very personal thing and should not be read by anyone but its owner.

______   ______   7. A child who asks lots of questions is considered a pest.

______   ______   8. If your attempt to be friendly to another person is rejected, you should stop trying.

______   ______   9. There is a big difference between privacy and secrecy.

______   ______   10. One reason why a father and son may not get along is that they are too much alike.

______   ______   11. A stubborn person is his or her own worst enemy.

______   ______   12. One does not have to be sad to cry.

CALL IT COURAGE

by Armstrong Sperry, Scholastic, 1940

Put a check on the line under AGREE if you agree with the statement. Put a check on the line under DISAGREE if you disagree with the statement.

AGREE   DISAGREE

______   ______   1. To be the son of an important leader is difficult, because too much is expected of you.

______   ______   2. Unreasonable fears are learned at an early age.

______   ______   3. Every human being fears something.

______   ______   4. A fearful person cannot be courageous.

______   ______   5. Nature can be a stronger enemy than a person.

______   ______   6. Being called a coward is not the worst thing that can happen to you.

______   ______   7. People who live on an island must depend on nature to survive.

______   ______   8. Cannibals exist only in stories.

______   ______   9. A dog can often be your best friend and companion.

______   ______   10. It is more important to satisfy yourself than to satisfy others.

______   ______   11. Fears can be conquered when they are faced head on.

______   ______   12. Despair and inaction go together.

CALL OF THE WILD

by Jack London, E. P. Dutton, 1968 (1903)

Put a check on the line under AGREE if you agree with the statement. Put a check on the line under DISAGREE if you disagree with the statement.

AGREE   DISAGREE

______   ______   1. A California ranch would be an ideal place to live.

______   ______   2. You should interfere if you see someone mistreating an animal.

______   ______   3. Experiencing snow for the first time would be frightening.

______   ______   4. Learning new habits can be very difficult.

______   ______   5. Stealing to survive is not morally wrong.

______   ______   6. Poise and control are essential if you want to carry out devious behavior.

______   ______   7. Brains may often win, rather than strength.

______   ______   8. The most important characteristic of a leader is the ability to listen.

______   ______   9. Beating an animal into submission is never necessary or justified.

______   ______   10. A dog may break its heart when it tries and fails.

______   ______   11. The Arctic holds many hardships for both people and dogs.

______   ______   12. Some animals take on the personalities of their owners.

CARRIE'S WAR

by Nina Bawden, Lippincott, 1973

Put a check on the line under AGREE if you agree with the statement. Put a check on the line under DISAGREE if you disagree with the statement.

AGREE   DISAGREE

______   ______   1. Ordinary citizens are as severely affected by war as are those who are fighting.

______   ______   2. Children are better off living with their own parents than being sent far away to live with strangers, even though their town may be bombed in wartime.

______   ______   3. A bully is a person with low self-esteem.

______   ______   4. Children should not be required to visit a person who is dying.

______   ______   5. The most difficult part of leaving home is adapting to the lifestyle of a new family.

______   ______   6. Kind people are born that way; they were not taught to be kind.

______   ______   7. Most children will welcome a physically or mentally handicapped child as a playmate.

______   ______   8. Wealthy people are happier than people of moderate means.

______   ______   9. A person who never leaves his or her home has a fear of other people.

______   ______   10. Some people can make life magical for others.

______   ______   11. In books, all witches are evil characters.

______   ______   12. Some people are natural born storytellers.

CASTLE IN THE ATTIC

by Elizabeth Winthrop, E. P. Dutton, 1981

Put a check on the line under AGREE if you agree with the statement. Put a check on the line under DISAGREE if you disagree with the statement.

AGREE   DISAGREE

_____   _____   1. One sign of growing up is demonstrating responsibility.

_____   _____   2. There is no good reason to hide another person's prized possessions.

_____   _____   3. The smallest kid in a class has to put up with a lot of teasing.

_____   _____   4. Daydreaming through class may result in creative ideas.

_____   _____   5. Sometimes it is wise not to be truthful with a friend.

_____   _____   6. An attic full of secrets would be a wonderful place to explore.

_____   _____   7. A person who never finishes a project is lazy.

_____   _____   8. Poor performance usually occurs when special people are watching.

_____   _____   9. Deliberately walking into danger is sometimes necessary.

_____   _____   10. It is tempting to stray from so-called a path when all your friends are doing it.

_____   _____   11. A person with a so-called heart of stone has known much hardship in his or her life.

_____   _____   12. The greatest power a human has is love.

CAT RUNNING

by Zilpha Keatley Snyder, Delacorte, 1994

Put a check on the line under AGREE if you agree with the statement. Put a check on the line under DISAGREE if you disagree with the statement.

AGREE   DISAGREE

______   ______   1. Parents are not always truthful about their reasons for not allowing certain behaviors.

______   ______   2. Some children are their own worst enemies.

______   ______   3. Stubborn people have few friends.

______   ______   4. Children can't help being prejudiced; they learn prejudice from their parents.

______   ______   5. During the Depression years, everyone was poor.

______   ______   6. Parents should have the final say on what their children wear.

______   ______   7. It is possible to be poor and not know it.

______   ______   8. There is less prejudice in today's world than there was during the Depression years.

______   ______   9. A special gift to a friend guarantees an enduring friendship.

______   ______   10. It is possible to gain respect for someone you dislike.

______   ______   11. The best way to deal with anger is to hit something.

______   ______   12. To be a refugee you do not have to come from another country.

CATHERINE, CALLED BIRDY

by Karen Cushman, Houghton Mifflin, 1994

Put a check on the line under AGREE if you agree with the statement. Put a check on the line under DISAGREE if you disagree with the statement.

AGREE   DISAGREE

_______   _______   1. Deciding what to do with one's life is not always easy.

_______   _______   2. People in our information age do not believe in superstitions.

_______   _______   3. Jealousy may lead to misery on the part of the jealous person.

_______   _______   4. Good deeds can often be misunderstood.

_______   _______   5. Life in a castle would be luxurious.

_______   _______   6. When guilt and anxiety mix, nothing can be accomplished.

_______   _______   7. People who mistreat children were themselves mistreated as children.

_______   _______   8. The mark of a lady is the dress she wears.

_______   _______   9. A forced marriage may result in happiness for both parties.

_______   _______   10. Patience, gentleness, and a willing heart can lead to success in achieving a goal.

_______   _______   11. One who is cruel to animals is cruel to people as well.

_______   _______   12. The most important thing you can do is to be true to yourself.

THE CAY

by Theodore Taylor, Doubleday, 1969

Put a check on the line under AGREE if you agree with the statement. Put a check on the line under DISAGREE if you disagree with the statement.

AGREE   DISAGREE

_______   _______   1. Living in a place without seasons would be boring.

_______   _______   2. Prejudice is learned at home.

_______   _______   3. The Earth provides all that is needed for human survival.

_______   _______   4. A blind person must have someone with him or her at all times.

_______   _______   5. Many innocent people are killed in wartime.

_______   _______   6. Leaders who try to conserve dwindling supplies of food and water are often resented.

_______   _______   7. Black cats harbor evil spirits.

_______   _______   8. Total dependence on a person leads to resentment.

_______   _______   9. Most people have greater ability than they think they have.

_______   _______   10. There are times when knowledge is more important than wisdom.

_______   _______   11. People from different backgrounds can learn a great deal from each other.

_______   _______   12. Most people fear the unknown.

CHARLIE AND THE CHOCOLATE FACTORY

by Roald Dahl, Alfred A. Knopf, 1973

Put a check on the line under AGREE if you agree with the statement. Put a check on the line under DISAGREE if you disagree with the statement.

AGREE   DISAGREE

_______   _______   1. A spoiled girl who screams until she gets what she wants will never be a happy person.

_______   _______   2. Poor families are always unhappy families.

_______   _______   3. It is okay to steal food for a hungry family.

_______   _______   4. Spies can shut down a business.

_______   _______   5. A chocolate factory would be filled with magic and secrets.

_______   _______   6. Receiving one candy bar a year for your birthday would be the best birthday present ever.

_______   _______   7. Some people are addicted to television; they cannot stop watching even if they don't like the program.

_______   _______   8. It is better to eat fresh fruits than to eat candy bars.

_______   _______   9. If you find money on the street, you should turn it in to the police.

_______   _______   10. It is hard for children to have a good relationship with their grandparents, because they are so far apart in age.

_______   _______   11. Some people act very differently at night than they do during the day.

_______   _______   12. Winning a prize is not always a good thing.

CHARLIE SKEDADDLE

by Patricia Beatty, William Morrow, 1987

Put a check on the line under AGREE if you agree with the statement. Put a check on the line under DISAGREE if you disagree with the statement.

AGREE   DISAGREE

_______   _______   1. Surviving as a gang member on the streets of New York is as dangerous as surviving on a battlefield.

_______   _______   2. For a young boy, being sent to prison is worse than joining an army that faces bloody battles.

_______   _______   3. A real battle is nothing like the glory young men envision.

_______   _______   4. Only a coward would run from the horror of a battlefield.

_______   _______   5. An opposing army would not make a prisoner of a very young boy.

_______   _______   6. Strangers are never to be trusted.

_______   _______   7. A deserter carries that shame for the rest of his or her life.

_______   _______   8. Once branded a coward, one can never become a hero in the eyes of others.

_______   _______   9. Soldiers are not the only people who know suffering in time of war.

_______   _______   10. Fighting is the only solution when both sides believe they are right.

_______   _______   11. A person of courage is never fearful.

_______   _______   12. The only way to survive in a big city is to become a member of a gang.

CHARLOTTE'S ROSE

by A. E. Cannon, Wendy Lamb Books, 2002

Put a check on the line under AGREE if you agree with the statement. Put a check on the line under DISAGREE if you disagree with the statement.

AGREE   DISAGREE

_____   _____   1. Pioneer families depended on each other far more than modern families do.

_____   _____   2. People traveled the Mormon Trail either on horseback or in horse-drawn wagons.

_____   _____   3. A person committed to a cause will never compromise.

_____   _____   4. Leaving one's home country for a new world is a fearful undertaking.

_____   _____   5. Never become attached to another human being, for one day the two of you will be separated.

_____   _____   6. When a woman dies in childbirth, the father should not be expected to take care of the baby.

_____   _____   7. A man who refuses to care for his newborn child should never be given the opportunity to do so when the child is older.

_____   _____   8. Throughout history many people have been persecuted for their religious beliefs, but this is not true today.

_____   _____   9. Making a drastic change in one's life requires a great deal of courage.

_____   _____   10. Even sad words may bring sweet comfort.

_____   _____   11. Get to know a stranger well before you offer the hand of friendship.

_____   _____   12. The more problems a family faces, the stronger it becomes.

CHILD OF THE OWL

by Laurence Yep, HarperCollins, 1977

Put a check on the line under AGREE if you agree with the statement. Put a check on the line under DISAGREE if you disagree with the statement.

AGREE   DISAGREE

______   ______   1. Compulsive gamblers can't help their addiction, regardless of the pain they bring to others.

______   ______   2. Moving often from one city to another is an exciting life for a child.

______   ______   3. Many Chinese Americans know nothing about their Chinese heritage.

______   ______   4. It is impossible for grandparents and grandchildren to understand each other, because they come from different generations.

______   ______   5. Senior citizens have much of value to share with the young.

______   ______   6. Race is often a factor in not being considered for a job for which one is qualified.

______   ______   7. Thieves often try to rationalize their crimes.

______   ______   8. It is impossible to forgive a person who injures a loved one.

______   ______   9. It is impossible for some people to stay in one place or keep a job.

______   ______   10. The legends of a people are handed down from generation to generation because they contain great wisdom.

______   ______   11. Most people wear a disguise, so that their true feelings are never expressed.

______   ______   12. Chinatown is a state of mind and heart.

COME SING, JIMMY JO

by Katherine Paterson, E. P. Dutton, 1985

Put a check on the line under AGREE if you agree with the statement. Put a check on the line under DISAGREE if you disagree with the statement.

AGREE   DISAGREE

——————   ——————   1. Professional singers may experience stage fright.

——————   ——————   2. Too many changes at one time are difficult to cope with.

——————   ——————   3. Leaving home, even with your parents, can be scary.

——————   ——————   4. The first day at a new school is exciting.

——————   ——————   5. Jealousy shows its face in many ways.

——————   ——————   6. A person without a friend is hard to get along with.

——————   ——————   7. Some performers just go through the motions.

——————   ——————   8. Upstaging a star leads to trouble.

——————   ——————   9. Pioneer neighbors often helped each other.

——————   ——————   10. It is easy to let someone put words in your mouth.

——————   ——————   11. Celebrities often hide their identity.

——————   ——————   12. People who show talent in any area should work to develop that talent.

CORALINE

by Neil Gaimon, HarperCollins, 2002

Put a check on the line under AGREE if you agree with the statement. Put a check on the line under DISAGREE if you disagree with the statement.

AGREE   DISAGREE

______   ______   1. A good parent may provide well for his or her children yet not spend any time with them.

______   ______   2. Constant boredom always leads to trouble.

______   ______   3. One should never explore strange surroundings alone.

______   ______   4. If something appears too good to be true, it probably is.

______   ______   5. Evil is often disguised as beauty and goodness.

______   ______   6. Too much curiosity may get you into big trouble.

______   ______   7. It is a foolish person who does not heed ominous warnings.

______   ______   8. Doing what you know you are not supposed to do means you don't believe there will be consequences.

______   ______   9. Some stones have special powers.

______   ______   10. It is never wise to challenge someone in authority.

______   ______   11. It would be no fun to get everything you wanted.

______   ______   12. Adults often label children's pleas for help as the result of an overactive imagination.

COUSINS

by Virginia Hamilton, Philomel, 1990

Put a check on the line under AGREE if you agree with the statement. Put a check on the line under DISAGREE if you disagree with the statement.

AGREE   DISAGREE

_______   _______   1. Being consumed with jealousy only hurts the person who is jealous.

_______   _______   2. A bulimic person can't help being bulimic and needs medical help to eat normally.

_______   _______   3. One should never swim in a fast-moving river.

_______   _______   4. A feeling of guilt, even though not justified, can make one ill.

_______   _______   5. Never wish to be like someone else; always be yourself.

_______   _______   6. Some games like "Dead as a Doornail" are very dangerous to play.

_______   _______   7. It is not possible to speed up time; you must live each minute as it comes.

_______   _______   8. It would be more fun to live under trees in the woods than to live in a house.

_______   _______   9. You can dislike a person yet want to be like that person.

_______   _______   10. Some days are pinned to our lives forever.

_______   _______   11. A girl without a father has a hard time being friends with a boy.

_______   _______   12. Always be ready to grasp an unexpected opportunity.

THE CRICKET IN TIMES SQUARE

by George Selden, Farrar, Straus & Giroux, 1960

Put a check on the line under AGREE if you agree with the statement. Put a check on the line under DISAGREE if you disagree with the statement.

AGREE   DISAGREE

———   ———   1. Many people keep crickets for pets.

———   ———   2. Life in the country is more satisfying than life in the city.

———   ———   3. You do not have to speak Italian to enjoy Italian music.

———   ———   4. Living away from home can make you feel happy and sad at the same time.

———   ———   5. It is very easy to get lost in a large city.

———   ———   6. One cannot operate an unprofitable business indefinitely.

———   ———   7. Only in a fantasy tale could a mouse, a cat, and a cricket become friends.

———   ———   8. A startling discovery may be either good or bad.

———   ———   9. A pet should never be kept in a cage.

———   ———   10. A true friend will keep you from doing things you should not do.

———   ———   11. It is not possible for a person to be a jinx.

———   ———   12. It is easy to forget your friends once you become famous.

CRISPIN: THE CROSS OF LEAD

by Avi, Hyperion Books, 2002

Put a check on the line under AGREE if you agree with the statement. Put a check on the line under DISAGREE if you disagree with the statement.

AGREE   DISAGREE

______   ______   1. A young boy alone in the world can't take care of himself.

______   ______   2. To be illiterate is to miss life's greatest joys.

______   ______   3. You should tell those in authority if you overhear a plot to do harm.

______   ______   4. Many people are accused of and jailed for crimes they did not commit.

______   ______   5. Moving out of the frying pan into the fire means that a dangerous situation is becoming less dangerous.

______   ______   6. Sometimes in a given situation there is no one who can be trusted.

______   ______   7. It is usually better not to tell all that you know.

______   ______   8. Not following orders can result in chaos.

______   ______   9. Protest meetings never result in positive action.

______   ______   10. Breaking a pledge may lead to feelings of guilt.

______   ______   11. It is possible for an enemy to become a friend.

______   ______   12. People in the Middle Ages were, for the most part, unfeeling and cruel.

THE DARK IS RISING

by Susan Cooper, Atheneum, 1974

Put a check on the line under AGREE if you agree with the statement. Put a check on the line under DISAGREE if you disagree with the statement.

AGREE   DISAGREE

_______   _______   1. Negative things in people's lives are caused by their own mistakes.

_______   _______   2. People who are prejudiced have chosen to accept the prejudices of their parents.

_______   _______   3. There have always been wars and there will always be wars, regardless of people's efforts to prevent them.

_______   _______   4. No matter how much people have, they will always want more.

_______   _______   5. It is better to take action than to trust to fate.

_______   _______   6. In the end, most people get the rewards they earn.

_______   _______   7. Most people who are unemployed could get a job.

_______   _______   8. Success depends mainly on being at the right place at the right time.

_______   _______   9. Some people are born to lead, others to follow.

_______   _______   10. Juvenile delinquents often choose as friends others who get into trouble.

_______   _______   11. If you look hard enough, you can find some good in everyone.

_______   _______   12. If you never try, you will never know if you can succeed.

DAVE AT NIGHT

by Gail Carson Levine, HarperCollins, 1999

Put a check on the line under AGREE if you agree with the statement. Put a check on the line under DISAGREE if you disagree with the statement.

AGREE   DISAGREE

_____   _____   1. There are no orphan asylums in the United States today.

_____   _____   2. No one wants to take a troublesome, noisy boy into his or her home.

_____   _____   3. Children are powerless against adults in authority.

_____   _____   4. It is not wrong to steal something that belongs to you.

_____   _____   5. All bullies are cowards at heart.

_____   _____   6. When a problem seems too big, run away.

_____   _____   7. Neighbors help each other more in poor than in rich neighborhoods.

_____   _____   8. All fortune-tellers are frauds. No one can tell the future.

_____   _____   9. A talent is useless unless it is developed.

_____   _____   10. Good things can always be found in bad surroundings.

_____   _____   11. The most difficult thing you have to do is to find your place in the world.

_____   _____   12. Any hardship can be endured if you are surrounded by good friends.

DEAR MR. HENSHAW

by Beverly Cleary, William Morrow, 1983

Put a check on the line under AGREE if you agree with the statement. Put a check on the line under DISAGREE if you disagree with the statement.

AGREE   DISAGREE

______   ______   1. It is fun to be the new kid at school.

______   ______   2. Children are loners because they choose to be.

______   ______   3. One way to get rid of anger is to take a long walk.

______   ______   4. Children need adults to listen to them.

______   ______   5. If you don't expect anything, you won't be disappointed.

______   ______   6. Everyone has at least one special talent.

______   ______   7. It is easier to write your thoughts than to speak them.

______   ______   8. Being alone at night is scary.

______   ______   9. It is foolish to wish for something you know won't happen.

______   ______   10. Some people never really grow up.

______   ______   11. An angry person is usually an unhappy person.

______   ______   12. Watching the ocean waves can be soothing.

THE DEVIL'S ARITHMETIC

by Jane Yolen, Viking, 1988

Put a check on the line under AGREE if you agree with the statement. Put a check on the line under DISAGREE if you disagree with the statement.

AGREE   DISAGREE

———   ———   1. Young people are often bored by family traditions.

———   ———   2. Events of the distant past have little effect on children's lives today.

———   ———   3. Recalling painful events of the past is foolish, since those events cannot be changed.

———   ———   4. People who say they know what will happen in the future are rarely believed.

———   ———   5. A law-abiding group of people would not be imprisoned simply because of their religion.

———   ———   6. A soldier who is ordered to hurt innocent people is justified in deserting.

———   ———   7. A warning of danger from a child is usually dismissed as the result of an over-active imagination.

———   ———   8. In World War II, six million Jews died at the hands of the Nazis.

———   ———   9. To truly understand a difficult situation, one must experience it.

———   ———   10. One who ignores the errors of the past is destined to repeat them.

———   ———   11. Children today should not be told about the Holocaust as it was too terrible a time in history.

———   ———   12. Throughout history, in the struggle between good and evil, good has always won.

DEW DROP DEAD: A SEBASTIAN BARTH MYSTERY

by James Howe, Macmillan, 1990

Put a check on the line under AGREE if you agree with the statement. Put a check on the line under DISAGREE if you disagree with the statement.

AGREE   DISAGREE

______   ______   1. A father should be the main support of a family.

______   ______   2. All professional writers suffer from writer's block at one time or another.

______   ______   3. Exploring an abandoned house can be dangerous.

______   ______   4. When children tell an unusual story, they are not likely to be believed.

______   ______   5. Circumstantial evidence has convicted innocent people of crimes they did not commit.

______   ______   6. Homeless people are homeless because they want to be.

______   ______   7. Homeless people don't work for a living.

______   ______   8. Most homeless people are mentally ill.

______   ______   9. It is dangerous to befriend a homeless person.

______   ______   10. It is impossible to care about people you don't know.

______   ______   11. When a father loses his job, tempers will flare in the family.

______   ______   12. Homeless people face many dangers every day.

DICEY'S SONG

by Cynthia Voight, Atheneum, 1983

Put a check on the line under AGREE if you agree with the statement. Put a check on the line under DISAGREE if you disagree with the statement.

AGREE   DISAGREE

______   ______   1. There may be very good reasons for a mother to abandon her children.

______   ______   2. At some time, everyone is forced to do something he or she does not want to do.

______   ______   3. A person who is stony-faced and uninvolved enjoys being a loner.

______   ______   4. There is never any justification for teasing and mocking another person.

______   ______   5. There may be good reasons for rejecting offers of friendship from others.

______   ______   6. Children who struggle with reading and math in the early grades will never do well in school.

______   ______   7. Some children deliberately do poor work in school in order to gain more friends.

______   ______   8. One has no defense when falsely accused of plagiarism by a teacher.

______   ______   9. Older people are often better at a game than the children who play it every day.

______   ______   10. Everyone is born with a special gift or talent that needs to be developed.

______   ______   11. An invitation can make you feel good, even if you turn it down.

______   ______   12. Often children are expected to take on adult responsibilities before they are ready.

A DOG CALLED KITTY

by Bill Wallace, Holiday House, 1980

Put a check on the line under AGREE if you agree with the statement. Put a check on the line under DISAGREE if you disagree with the statement.

AGREE   DISAGREE

_____   _____   1. Children are born with a fear of animals.

_____   _____   2. Arguing over a game is foolish.

_____   _____   3. It takes work to make a dream come true.

_____   _____   4. Sometimes it's hard to avoid a fight.

_____   _____   5. Some people let fear run their lives.

_____   _____   6. Worry can keep one from going to sleep.

_____   _____   7. Only cruel people abandon pets on a country road.

_____   _____   8. Sometimes it's wise to pen up a dog.

_____   _____   9. A hero is a person who is always brave.

_____   _____   10. Keeping a secret is easy.

_____   _____   11. When someone's mind is made up, it can't be changed.

_____   _____   12. Little brothers can be a lot of trouble.

THE DOLLHOUSE MURDERS

by Betty Ren Wright, Holiday House, 1983

Put a check on the line under AGREE if you agree with the statement. Put a check
on the line under DISAGREE if you disagree with the statement.

AGREE   DISAGREE

_____   _____   1. Many older children resent having to look after a younger brother or sister.

_____   _____   2. You should never lose your temper with your parents.

_____   _____   3. Night noises in the country may be frightening.

_____   _____   4. The library is the best place to go for information.

_____   _____   5. No one wants to live in a house where a murder has taken place.

_____   _____   6. Unjust accusations are made by those who don't know the facts of a situation.

_____   _____   7. It is possible to feel angry and guilty at the same time.

_____   _____   8. An unwanted guest can spoil a party.

_____   _____   9. It is possible for a doll to cry and to move.

_____   _____   10. Apologizing is easy when you know you are in the wrong.

_____   _____   11. Some people are not responsible for their own actions.

_____   _____   12. A murder mystery and a violent storm go together.

THE DOOR IN THE WALL

by Marguerite de Angeli, Doubleday, 1949

Put a check on the line under AGREE if you agree with the statement. Put a check on the line under DISAGREE if you disagree with the statement.

AGREE   DISAGREE

_____   _____   1. Being forced to live up to your family's expectations is unreasonable.

_____   _____   2. The best thing to do when you are in a bad temper is to smash something.

_____   _____   3. A boy who cannot walk has a right to feel sorry for himself.

_____   _____   4. If you have to give up a dream of what to do with your life, don't substitute another dream.

_____   _____   5. If a kind deed is rebuffed, the deed is not likely to be repeated.

_____   _____   6. Creating something with your hands is always satisfying.

_____   _____   7. Sleeping in Mother Nature's arms means depending on nature to make you well.

_____   _____   8. Peace is seldom found in a rebellious nature.

_____   _____   9. When you come to a stone wall, if you look long enough you will find a door in it.

_____   _____   10. Anyone can NOT do it means that anything worthwhile takes effort.

_____   _____   11. Pretending to be something you are not is the same as telling a lie.

_____   _____   12. It is not possible to be fearful and brave at the same time.

THE DOUBLE LIFE OF POCAHONTAS

by Jean Fritz, Putnam's, 1983

Put a check on the line under AGREE if you agree with the statement. Put a check on the line under DISAGREE if you disagree with the statement.

AGREE   DISAGREE

_______   _______ 1. When strangers come to a new land, they are viewed with suspicion.

_______   _______ 2. Hungry people will trade anything they own for food.

_______   _______ 3. A good leader will put his people's needs before his own.

_______   _______ 4. When people fight among themselves, nothing gets accomplished.

_______   _______ 5. Living in two different worlds can be exciting.

_______   _______ 6. When a whole village is starving, nothing can be done.

_______   _______ 7. There is always a reason to stage an attack on other people.

_______   _______ 8. One who is forced to listen to strange beliefs will become resentful.

_______   _______ 9. Be wary of smiling faces; you may be walking into a trap.

_______   _______ 10. Native Americans and settlers never helped each other.

_______   _______ 11. You can respect another person's beliefs without agreeing with those beliefs.

_______   _______ 12. Learning another language is easy if you are highly motivated to learn it.

DR. DREDD'S WAGON OF WONDERS

by Bill Brittain, HarperCollins, 1987

Put a check on the line under AGREE if you agree with the statement. Put a check on the line under DISAGREE if you disagree with the statement.

AGREE   DISAGREE

_____   _____   1. Nothing can be done to lessen the effects of a drought.

_____   _____   2. Nothing is ever free; everything has a cost of some kind.

_____   _____   3. Never trust a stranger who makes extravagant promises.

_____   _____   4. Always know what a job will cost before it is started.

_____   _____   5. There may be good reasons for rejecting offers of friendship from others.

_____   _____   6. Children who struggle with reading and math in the early grades will never do well in school.

_____   _____   7. Some children deliberately do poor work in school in order to gain more friends.

_____   _____   8. One has no defense when falsely accused of plagiarism by a teacher.

_____   _____   9. Older people are often better at a game than the children who play it every day.

_____   _____   10. Everyone is born with a special gift or talent that needs to be developed.

_____   _____   11. An invitation can make you feel good, even if you turn it down.

_____   _____   12. Often children are expected to take on adult responsibilities before they are ready.

THE DRAGON'S BOY

by Jane Yolen, HarperCollins, 1990

Put a check on the line under AGREE if you agree with the statement. Put a check on the line under DISAGREE if you disagree with the statement.

AGREE   DISAGREE

_____   _____   1. You can be a part of a family yet feel that you do not truly belong.

_____   _____   2. Being ignored by other children is worse than being picked on.

_____   _____   3. You should never explore alone the hidden dangers in a cave.

_____   _____   4. If given the choice of a gift of gold or wisdom, people everywhere would choose the gold.

_____   _____   5. To gain the respect of others, carry a weapon.

_____   _____   6. A forced friendship with someone you don't like is too high a price to pay for something you desperately want.

_____   _____   7. True wisdom comes from reading between the lines.

_____   _____   8. A person acting alone is less likely to treat others badly than if that person acts as part of a group.

_____   _____   9. You should never forgive a person who deliberately deceives you.

_____   _____   10. Most people can show courage and bravery if the cause is just.

_____   _____   11. A great leader cares for and understands those he must lead.

_____   _____   12. People like to show off any new possession they have acquired.

THE EGYPT GAME

by Zilpha Keatley Snyder, Atheneum, 1967

Put a check on the line under AGREE if you agree with the statement. Put a check on the line under DISAGREE if you disagree with the statement.

AGREE   DISAGREE

_____   _____   1. Children from very different backgrounds can become good friends.

_____   _____   2. Lonely children often live in imaginary worlds that they create.

_____   _____   3. An imaginary game can become more real than everyday life.

_____   _____   4. It is easier to accuse someone of a crime than to prove his or her guilt.

_____   _____   5. People should be judged by what they do rather than by what they say.

_____   _____   6. When you meet someone for the first time, your first impressions are usually right.

_____   _____   7. In most friendships, one person is the leader and the other is a follower.

_____   _____   8. There are times when it is necessary for a mother to abandon her children.

_____   _____   9. A real family does not have to consist of a mother, a father, and children.

_____   _____   10. Jumping to conclusions usually results in wrong answers.

_____   _____   11. To accomplish a big task, teamwork is essential.

_____   _____   12. Students today would not be interested in a game based on ancient Egypt.

ELLA ENCHANTED

by Gail Carson Levine, HarperCollins, 1997

Put a check on the line under AGREE if you agree with the statement. Put a check on the line under DISAGREE if you disagree with the statement.

AGREE   DISAGREE

_____   _____   1. In the world of enchantment, a gift of obedience would not be welcomed.

_____   _____   2. One who must always obey others can never truly be himself or herself.

_____   _____   3. No one enjoys having a rebel around; you never know what the rebel will do next.

_____   _____   4. A marriage arranged by parents is likely to be successful.

_____   _____   5. One should never end a friendship simply because one is ordered to do so.

_____   _____   6. Jealousy may lead a person to commit cruel acts.

_____   _____   7. Most people have unusual powers that have never been developed.

_____   _____   8. One cannot be forced into doing good; one must choose to do good.

_____   _____   9. Some people are born with a natural ability to learn other languages.

_____   _____   10. People cannot take advantage of you unless you let them.

_____   _____   11. One who is forced to obey every command may bring harm to loved ones.

_____   _____   12. Magic that cannot be explained is found only in fantasy tales.

ENCYCLOPEDIA BROWN, BOY DETECTIVE

by Donald Sobol, E. P. Dutton, 1963

Put a check on the line under AGREE if you agree with the statement. Put a check on the line under DISAGREE if you disagree with the statement.

AGREE   DISAGREE

_____   _____   1. A ten-year-old can solve a mystery.

_____   _____   2. Doing crossword puzzles is good for your brain.

_____   _____   3. When the facts don't fit, look for more facts.

_____   _____   4. The dictionary is a good book for pleasure reading.

_____   _____   5. When a bully is after you, stop and fight.

_____   _____   6. You cannot be friends with someone who is smarter than you.

_____   _____   7. There would never be an open newspaper in a blind man's room.

_____   _____   8. Wearing a valuable diamond necklace is foolish.

_____   _____   9. Sometimes the police arrest the wrong person.

_____   _____   10. Leaving a package unattended is asking for trouble.

_____   _____   11. A good alibi is one that is true.

_____   _____   12. Losing something that belongs to someone else is irresponsible.

THE ETERNAL SPRING OF MR. ITO

by Sheila Garrigue, Bradbury, 1985

Put a check on the line under AGREE if you agree with the statement. Put a check on the line under DISAGREE if you disagree with the statement.

AGREE   DISAGREE

_____   _____   1. Starting a new life in a new country is very difficult.

_____   _____   2. It is possible to see beauty that is not evident.

_____   _____   3. It is important to keep up the traditions of one's culture.

_____   _____   4. The expression "mob rule" means that a country is ruled by more than one person.

_____   _____   5. Most people desperately want to be needed.

_____   _____   6. A so-called thick silence usually implies that something unpleasant has been said.

_____   _____   7. In World War II, innocent Japanese people were treated like criminals.

_____   _____   8. Sharing a secret is okay when it means a better life for someone.

_____   _____   9. There is no point in doing schoolwork if you are in prison.

_____   _____   10. A deception is not wrong if good can come of it.

_____   _____   11. Understanding another person's views does not mean you agree with them.

_____   _____   12. Keeping a promise can be very difficult.

EVERYTHING ON A WAFFLE

by Polly Horvath, Farrar, Straus & Giroux, 2001

Put a check on the line under AGREE if you agree with the statement. Put a check on the line under DISAGREE if you disagree with the statement.

AGREE   DISAGREE

————   ————   1. Some people attract trouble wherever they go.

————   ————   2. It is possible to know something is true without proof or reason.

————   ————   3. An accident often leads to a positive result.

————   ————   4. Fish would be delicious if served on a waffle.

————   ————   5. A problem does not seem nearly as overwhelming if you can share it with someone else.

————   ————   6. Making quick judgments about people you have just met is a mistake.

————   ————   7. Patrons are always pleased when a restaurant serves a little something extra with the meal.

————   ————   8. It is much harder not to blame people than to blame them when they make a mistake.

————   ————   9. Children always know when they are in the company of a person who does not like children.

————   ————   10. Many people have a sixth sense and see things that others do not see.

————   ————   11. There are no miracles in life today.

————   ————   12. It is a mistake to try to make something wonderful even better.

EVERYWHERE

by Bruce Brooks, HarperCollins, 1990

Put a check on the line under AGREE if you agree with the statement. Put a check on the line under DISAGREE if you disagree with the statement.

AGREE   DISAGREE

_____   _____   1. All of the action in a novel can take place in one day.

_____   _____   2. It is possible to qualify to become a nurse over the course of one summer.

_____   _____   3. Children of one race expect to be rejected by children of a different race.

_____   _____   4. Heart attacks are always fatal in old people.

_____   _____   5. The soul of a human being can be traded for the soul of an animal.

_____   _____   6. There is never a good reason to kill a wild animal.

_____   _____   7. One can be smart and gullible at the same time.

_____   _____   8. People believe foolish things because they want to believe them.

_____   _____   9. Objects may trigger positive memories of people we care about.

_____   _____   10. You should never trick someone into believing a lie.

_____   _____   11. There are no miracles in life today.

_____   _____   12. Pretending to be what you are not may bring harm to others.

THE FACE ON THE MILK CARTON

by Caroline Cooney, Bantam Books, 1991

Put a check on the line under AGREE if you agree with the statement. Put a check on the line under DISAGREE if you disagree with the statement.

AGREE   DISAGREE

______   ______   1. Learning you are not who you thought you were can be very frightening.

______   ______   2. A teenager is not old enough to be told family secrets.

______   ______   3. A family album with no baby pictures may lead to questions and to disturbing answers.

______   ______   4. A boring life is better than a life with more questions than answers.

______   ______   5. All parents are concerned about their teens' driving.

______   ______   6. Teens welcome the rules that parents insist must be followed.

______   ______   7. If parents are untruthful on one topic, they can never be believed on any other.

______   ______   8. More often than not the truth can hurt.

______   ______   9. Keeping a diary can be therapeutic.

______   ______   10. The best way to keep from thinking disturbing thoughts is to keep busy.

______   ______   11. A lawyer can untangle confusion if he or she has all the facts.

______   ______   12. One of the handiest things you can have is a sympathetic ear.

FAIR WEATHER

by Richard Peck, Dial, 2001

Put a check on the line under AGREE if you agree with the statement. Put a check on the line under DISAGREE if you disagree with the statement.

AGREE   DISAGREE

_____   _____   1. Some people never set foot outside the town where they were born.

_____   _____   2. Country people are not as smart as city people.

_____   _____   3. Younger brothers are a bother and should never be taken on a trip.

_____   _____   4. Grandparents should not give advice, because they are out of touch with the modern world.

_____   _____   5. In 1893, the fastest way to travel was by train.

_____   _____   6. A kind deed may lead to bad results.

_____   _____   7. The electric light was the greatest, most useful invention of all time.

_____   _____   8. You have to declare independence from your peers before you can take that first step toward yourself.

_____   _____   9. Many people are afraid of new inventions and want nothing to do with them,

_____   _____   10. Living in 1893 would have been an exciting adventure.

_____   _____   11. Some grandparents get into more trouble than their grandchildren.

_____   _____   12. The development of technology may lead to drastic changes in people's lives.

A FAMILY APART

by Joan Lowery Nixon, Bantam Books, 1987

Put a check on the line under AGREE if you agree with the statement. Put a check on the line under DISAGREE if you disagree with the statement.

AGREE   DISAGREE

————   ————   1. Only a cruel mother sends her children away.

————   ————   2. Going on a long train journey is exciting.

————   ————   3. It is often difficult to do what needs to be done.

————   ————   4. Stealing food is okay if a family is hungry.

————   ————   5. Only a foolish girl pretends to be a boy.

————   ————   6. A good story can calm frightened children.

————   ————   7. Brothers and sisters should never be separated and sent to different homes.

————   ————   8. If a law hurts people, it should be broken.

————   ————   9. A mother's love can be shown in many ways.

————   ————   10. Becoming part of a new family is very difficult.

————   ————   11. The reasons for people's actions are not always clear.

————   ————   12. It hurts to be the last person chosen.

THE FAMILY UNDER THE BRIDGE

by Natalie Savage Carlson, Houghton Mifflin, 1959

Put a check on the line under AGREE if you agree with the statement. Put a check on the line under DISAGREE if you disagree with the statement.

AGREE   DISAGREE

______   ______   1. Most people are homeless because they choose to be.

______   ______   2. Fortune-tellers are frauds who make money out of people's wishes.

______   ______   3. It is possible to survive in the winter by living under a bridge.

______   ______   4. A child's best companion is a dog.

______   ______   5. Children who don't have to go to school are lucky.

______   ______   6. You should ignore a homeless person begging for money on the streets.

______   ______   7. Making holiday wishes is foolish when no money is available.

______   ______   8. A hungry person should not be punished for stealing food.

______   ______   9. Helping others is the best way to help yourself.

______   ______   10. Being unable to read or write would not be a problem for most people.

______   ______   11. Well-meaning people often do more harm than good.

______   ______   12. A person who appears to be cross may have a heart of gold.

FANTASTIC MR. FOX

by Roald Dahl, Alfred A. Knopf, 2002

Put a check on the line under AGREE if you agree with the statement. Put a check on the line under DISAGREE if you disagree with the statement.

AGREE   DISAGREE

______   ______   1. Farmers consider wildlife to be a nuisance.

______   ______   2. A fox is the farmer's worst enemy.

______   ______   3. One should never shoot a wild creature.

______   ______   4. Stereotypes exist only in literature.

______   ______   5. It takes more than one person to solve a problem.

______   ______   6. No matter how carefully plans are made, something will always go wrong.

______   ______   7. A fox can dig faster than a human.

______   ______   8. There is always one person who cannot be trusted with a secret.

______   ______   9. A fox has as much right to kill a chicken as a human being has to kill a deer.

______   ______   10. Some people are just plain mean spirited and will never change.

______   ______   11. All wildlife is a part of nature and should be protected.

______   ______   12. Foxhunting is a tradition among many wealthy families and should be continued.

THE FIRST FOUR YEARS

by Laura Ingalls Wilder, HarperCollins, 1971

Put a check on the line under AGREE if you agree with the statement. Put a check on the line under DISAGREE if you disagree with the statement.

AGREE   DISAGREE

_______   _______   1. One reason to hurry a wedding is to get the crops harvested.

_______   _______   2. Nature can be a farmer's worst enemy.

_______   _______   3. More bad things than good things happen throughout life.

_______   _______   4. When the odds are against you, don't try to win.

_______   _______   5. Pioneer women had a harder workday than pioneer men.

_______   _______   6. When a farmer's crop fails, he should leave the farm and find a different way to make a living.

_______   _______   7. Sometimes doing your best isn t good enough.

_______   _______   8. Fresh air and sunshine can cure depression.

_______   _______   9. When pioneers fell ill, there were no doctors or medicines to help them.

_______   _______   10. Hearing wolves howl at night means bad luck.

_______   _______   11. Breaking a promise means your word can never be trusted.

_______   _______   12. Books were useless to homesteaders since they did not know how to read.

FOG MAGIC

by Julia L. Sauer, Viking, 1971

Put a check on the line under AGREE if you agree with the statement. Put a check on the line under DISAGREE if you disagree with the statement.

AGREE   DISAGREE

_______   _______   1. Fog is like magic. It keeps you safe and always has something hidden in it.

_______   _______   2. If a lady dressed in taffeta, riding in a surrey, asked you to go for a ride, it would probably be a Halloween prank.

_______   _______   3. The purpose of a foghorn is to let people in coastal villages know the time.

_______   _______   4. One can visit an earlier time or place only in the imagination.

_______   _______   5. Magic can only happen when there is a very thick fog.

_______   _______   6. Taking cargo that is not yours from a wrecked ship is the same as stealing.

_______   _______   7. The best thing to do if falsely accused of a crime is to run away.

_______   _______   8. If you do not reach a self-determined goal, set a different goal for yourself.

_______   _______   9. There are no such things as ghosts.

_______   _______   10. People who refuse to speak simply have nothing to say.

_______   _______   11. "Looking ahead is something we do with our hearts."

_______   _______   12. "Living and dying are such natural things that one shouldn't be any more sorrowful than the other."

THE FORGOTTEN DOOR

by Alexander Key, Westminster, 1965

Put a check on the line under AGREE if you agree with the statement. Put a check on the line under DISAGREE if you disagree with the statement.

AGREE   DISAGREE

_____   _____   1. Not knowing who you are can be scary.

_____   _____   2. Having a visitor from another world is impossible.

_____   _____   3. People fear those who are more powerful than themselves.

_____   _____   4. A world without fear and hate is possible.

_____   _____   5. Sensing others feelings can make one uncomfortable.

_____   _____   6. Some people can communicate with wild animals.

_____   _____   7. Some people can read minds.

_____   _____   8. It is possible to learn a new language in one day.

_____   _____   9. Sometimes being truthful is not wise.

_____   _____   10. When rumors begin, they spread rapidly.

_____   _____   11. It is possible that there is life on other planets.

_____   _____   12. Sometimes we do good things for the wrong reasons.

FOURTH GRADE RATS

by Jerry Spinelli, Scholastic, 1991

Put a check on the line under AGREE if you agree with the statement. Put a check on the line under DISAGREE if you disagree with the statement.

AGREE   DISAGREE

_______   _______   1. Growing up can sometimes be painful.

_______   _______   2. Making fun of another person is okay if that person laughs with you.

_______   _______   3. When a bully takes your lunchbox, fight to get it back.

_______   _______   4. Pushing little kids off the swings shows that you are grown up.

_______   _______   5. Brothers and sisters can be good friends.

_______   _______   6. The best way to cheer people up is to make funny faces at them.

_______   _______   7. Mothers and messy rooms don't get along.

_______   _______   8. Confronting a bully would be a test of courage.

_______   _______   9. Little sisters like to tell tales.

_______   _______   10. When a friend acts strangely, it is best to ignore the strange behavior.

_______   _______   11. When you have a rotten time at a party it is your own fault.

_______   _______   12. Never say you are sorry if you don't mean it.

FRINDLE

by Andrew Clements, Simon & Schuster, 1996

Put a check on the line under AGREE if you agree with the statement. Put a check on the line under DISAGREE if you disagree with the statement.

AGREE   DISAGREE

_____   _____   1. The best way to start the day is to make a list of what needs to be done.

_____   _____   2. Troublemakers act up because they crave attention.

_____   _____   3. A teacher or parent with eyes like thunderclouds should be avoided.

_____   _____   4. Now that computers have spellcheck, dictionaries are no longer needed.

_____   _____   5. When homework is overwhelming, ignore it.

_____   _____   6. People with big ideas usually want someone else to carry them out.

_____   _____   7. When a teacher asks for a conference, it means trouble ahead.

_____   _____   8. Disrupting a class is not wrong if it is done for a good reason.

_____   _____   9. A home visit from the school principal means you are in big trouble.

_____   _____   10. A phony laugh is always followed by a lie.

_____   _____   11. When the unexpected happens, go with the flow.

_____   _____   12. Many words change their meanings over time.

FROM THE MIXED UP FILES OF
MRS. BASIL E. FRANKWEILER

by E. L. Konigsburg, Macmillan, 1967

Put a check on the line under AGREE if you agree with the statement. Put a check on the line under DISAGREE if you disagree with the statement.

AGREE   DISAGREE

_____   _____   1. Some children are ignored by the rest of the family.

_____   _____   2. Life for most children is nothing but enduring tyranny and following orders.

_____   _____   3. Running away from home will not solve the problems of an unhappy child.

_____   _____   4. People who complement each other should stick together.

_____   _____   5. A big city holds many dangers for a child alone.

_____   _____   6. A museum holds many mysteries.

_____   _____   7. Some people will not change their minds, regardless of the facts.

_____   _____   8. It is more fun to be different than to try to fit in with the crowd.

_____   _____   9. It is better to spend money on things you enjoy than to save for a rainy day.

_____   _____   10. Museums are very boring places.

_____   _____   11. A house with very few rooms may cost a lot of money.

_____   _____   12. Determination is more important than knowledge in solving a mystery.

FUDGE-A-MANIA

by *Judy Blume,* E. P. Dutton, 1990

Put a check on the line under AGREE if you agree with the statement. Put a check on the line under DISAGREE if you disagree with the statement.

AGREE   DISAGREE

_______   _______   1. Little brothers exist for one reason, to drive big brothers crazy.

_______   _______   2. It is hard to like someone who flaunts his or her knowledge.

_______   _______   3. Sharing a house with another family means trouble.

_______   _______   4. Those times when you really want to do your best seem to be the times when you are at your worst.

_______   _______   5. A grandmother doing cartwheels would be an embarrassing sight.

_______   _______   6. It is very hard to be the oldest child in a family.

_______   _______   7. Often people who mean well cause a lot of damage.

_______   _______   8. Young children often have unrealistic expectations.

_______   _______   9. Writing a book is easy; you just jot down your ideas.

_______   _______   10. A dog always knows when a person is afraid of dogs.

_______   _______   11. Teachers who let leaders choose teams are setting some children up for a hurtful experience.

_______   _______   12. There are many valid reasons for a person never to smile.

THE GADGET WAR

by Betsy Duffey, Viking, 1991

Put a check on the line under AGREE if you agree with the statement. Put a check on the line under DISAGREE if you disagree with the statement.

AGREE   DISAGREE

_______   _______   1. There is a big difference between laughing with someone and laughing at someone.

_______   _______   2. To see the potential in anything, one must create a mental image.

_______   _______   3. Rivalry among individuals or groups is not necessarily a bad thing.

_______   _______   4. Messy experiments can lead to useful discoveries.

_______   _______   5. It is never wise to say no to a teacher.

_______   _______   6. Getting even does not always bring satisfaction.

_______   _______   7. Inventors don't see the world as others see it.

_______   _______   8. A summons to the principal's office always means trouble.

_______   _______   9. Accepting blame for wrongdoing is a sign of maturity.

_______   _______   10. Only a very mature person can laugh at himself or herself.

_______   _______   11. The best solution to any war is a truce.

_______   _______   12. An inventor combines available objects in new ways to meet specific needs.

GATHERING BLUE

by Lois Lowry, Houghton Mifflin, 2000

Put a check on the line under AGREE if you agree with the statement. Put a check on the line under DISAGREE if you disagree with the statement.

AGREE   DISAGREE

_______   _______   1. A society that rejects members who are in some way deformed should never exist.

_______   _______   2. A comfortable life can be a form of imprisonment.

_______   _______   3. Without memories, life would be meaningless.

_______   _______   4. Without kindness and compassion, no society could exist.

_______   _______   5. Everyone is born with a particular talent that needs to be nurtured.

_______   _______   6. Fear causes one to shut down in both mind and body.

_______   _______   7. True art is self-expression carried to its highest level.

_______   _______   8. The best way to deal with a bully is to ignore him or her.

_______   _______   9. Many people in pain are stronger than those who have no pain.

_______   _______   10. One cannot be brave if one is afraid.

_______   _______   11. The most important quality in a friend is kindness.

_______   _______   12. It is possible not to be free, even if you live in an unlocked room.

GEORGE WASHINGTON'S SOCKS

by Elvira Woodruff, Scholastic, 1992

Put a check on the line under AGREE if you agree with the statement. Put a check on the line under DISAGREE if you disagree with the statement.

AGREE   DISAGREE

1. Never eat something on your plate that you don't like.

2. Little sisters can be a joy to have around.

3. Acting out an incident from history can be fun.

4. History is boring.

5. It is possible to feel wonder and fear at the same time.

6. A present-day man who claims to be George Washington must be mentally ill.

7. When a friend needs your help, never hesitate to respond.

8. Some day it may be possible to go back in time.

9. The most important quality of a leader is inflexibility.

10. When an army plunders, it is out of control.

11. When things seem darkest, something good usually happens.

12. An impossible situation can always be dealt with.

THE GIVER

by Lois Lowry, Houghton Mifflin, 1994

Put a check on the line under AGREE if you agree with the statement. Put a check on the line under DISAGREE if you disagree with the statement.

AGREE   DISAGREE

1. In future, society will eliminate all pain, fear, war, and hatred.

2. If everyone in a community looks and acts the same, there can be no prejudice.

3. Instead of choosing your life's work, it would be better to have it chosen for you according to your abilities and interests.

4. Life should always be as convenient and pleasant as possible.

5. A world without color could not exist.

6. Memories make life richer and more meaningful, even if some of the memories are unpleasant.

7. One who does not experience suffering can never know real joy.

8. It would be a better world if humans could see through the eyes of others.

9. A person who sees life differently from others is usually rejected by the society in which he or she lives.

10. Most older people are very wise and should be listened to.

11. It would be pleasant to live a life in which everything is planned and organized and there are no surprises.

12. Without imagination, there would be a complete halt in every field of human endeavor.

GOING THROUGH THE GATE

by Janet Anderson, E. P. Dutton, 1997

Put a check on the line under AGREE if you agree with the statement. Put a check on the line under DISAGREE if you disagree with the statement.

AGREE   DISAGREE

______   ______   1. Children in a one-room rural school learn more and faster than children in large city schools.

______   ______   2. Graduation is always a time of joy for graduates and their families.

______   ______   3. A teacher who rules with an iron hand is highly respected.

______   ______   4. A vegetarian diet is the best diet for human beings.

______   ______   5. It is foolish not to heed warnings of danger.

______   ______   6. It would be exciting to become a wild creature for one day.

______   ______   7. Not following the rules may lead to near-fatal results.

______   ______   8. All vegetarians strongly object to the killing of animals for food.

______   ______   9. Some teachers are so powerful that even parents are afraid of them.

______   ______   10. Some graduations are so complex that it takes a year to prepare for them.

______   ______   11. Every choice has a consequence.

______   ______   12. Everyone is better off not knowing what the future holds.

GRASSHOPPER SUMMER

by Ann Turner, Macmillan, 1989

Put a check on the line under AGREE if you agree with the statement. Put a check on the line under DISAGREE if you disagree with the statement.

AGREE   DISAGREE

______   ______   1. Giving up life on a comfortable farm for a long, hard journey to the West is foolish.

______   ______   2. Living in a sod house is like living in a grave.

______   ______   3. An endless prairie is empty and unwelcoming.

______   ______   4. Spying on someone is the lowest of the low.

______   ______   5. Holding on to bad things that happen guarantees a miserable life.

______   ______   6. It is useless to try to fight with someone who won't talk.

______   ______   7. Leaving the only home you have ever known may be the worst experience of your life.

______   ______   8. It is foolish to think too much about the hard things in life.

______   ______   9. Everyone needs time to be alone.

______   ______   10. Just when things seem darkest, good things happen.

______   ______   11. Moving to a new area changes the way you think.

______   ______   12. At some time in life, everyone will accomplish something he or she did not think was possible.

THE GREAT BRAIN

by John D. Fitzgerald, Doubleday, 1967

Put a check on the line under AGREE if you agree with the statement. Put a check on the line under DISAGREE if you disagree with the statement.

AGREE   DISAGREE

_______   _______   1. One of the greatest inventions of all time is the safety pin.

_______   _______   2. Selling something is easy if you believe in your product.

_______   _______   3. It is wrong to eavesdrop on another person's conversation.

_______   _______   4. Brainy kids at school are not accepted by other students.

_______   _______   5. The only thing worse than getting the silent treatment is being grounded.

_______   _______   6. Feelings are more difficult than money to share with another person.

_______   _______   7. Adapting to a totally new way of life takes a long time.

_______   _______   8. To receive charity is more difficult than to give it.

_______   _______   9. Pride is justifiable when a difficult task is accomplished.

_______   _______   10. The greatest gift one can give is to be a good listener.

_______   _______   11. Getting even does not usually lead to satisfaction.

_______   _______   12. Inattention is the principal cause of accidents.

THE GREAT GILLY HOPKINS

by Katherine Paterson, HarperCollins, 1978

Put a check on the line under AGREE if you agree with the statement. Put a check on the line under DISAGREE if you disagree with the statement.

AGREE   DISAGREE

______   ______   1. Some children are completely unmanageable.

______   ______   2. It is natural to feel anger when you believe you are not wanted.

______   ______   3. The best way to show resentment is to ignore those around you.

______   ______   4. Smart people don't need to cuss because they have larger vocabularies to draw on.

______   ______   5. Adults in authority should seek to find the reasons for a child's unacceptable behavior.

______   ______   6. It is okay to keep found money if no one knows it is lost.

______   ______   7. It is sometimes necessary to justify an opinion you don't really hold.

______   ______   8. Unkind words can be more painful than physical blows.

______   ______   9. Anger can bring people closer together.

______   ______   10. Passing judgment on others is easy; passing judgment on yourself is difficult.

______   ______   11. It is easy to take advantage of someone when you have that person's trust.

______   ______   12. Expecting good things in life all the time will make them happen.

THE GREY KING

by Susan Cooper, Atheneum, 1975

Put a check on the line under AGREE if you agree with the statement. Put a check on the line under DISAGREE if you disagree with the statement.

AGREE   DISAGREE

______   ______   1. An immortal being can become ill.

______   ______   2. Even today, dark forces seek to dominate the world.

______   ______   3. People known as albinos exist only in fantasy literature.

______   ______   4. In any hero's quest, there are numerous obstacles to overcome.

______   ______   5. Fires and landslides are acts of nature and are not caused by evil forces at work.

______   ______   6. In a mythic world, anything can happen.

______   ______   7. In the vastness of the universe, human beings are insignificant.

______   ______   8. There are many tasks that cannot be accomplished by one person alone.

______   ______   9. Facing difficult trials can bring people closer together.

______   ______   10. A farm is the best place to recuperate from an illness.

______   ______   11. Some problems are so complex they defy solution.

______   ______   12. Most fantasy literature is based on Arthurian legends and Welsh mythology.

HARRIET SPIES AGAIN

by Louise Fitzhugh and Helen Ericson, Delacorte, 2002

Put a check on the line under AGREE if you agree with the statement. Put a check on the line under DISAGREE if you disagree with the statement.

AGREE   DISAGREE

———   ———   1. The ability to look at things closely is a talent.

———   ———   2. Too much curiosity can get one into big trouble.

———   ———   3. Spying on another person is always wrong.

———   ———   4. A good author captures the reader's attention on the first page.

———   ———   5. It is possible for a parent to live in a house with a child and yet be an absent parent.

———   ———   6. Be careful what you write. Someone else might read it.

———   ———   7. It is possible to admire someone you don't like.

———   ———   8. Parents understand their childen far better than the children think they do.

———   ———   9. You cannot relive the past.

———   ———   10. Some people are too complicated to understand.

———   ———   11. Good memories should be cherished but should not dominate one's thinking.

———   ———   12. Statements of prejudice against any cultural group are allowed under the U.S. Constitution.

HARRY POTTER AND THE CHAMBER OF SECRETS

by J. K. Rowling, Scholastic, 1999

Put a check on the line under AGREE if you agree with the statement. Put a check on the line under DISAGREE if you disagree with the statement.

AGREE   DISAGREE

_______ _______ 1. A wise person makes choices to shape his or her life rather than waiting for life to shape itself.

_______ _______ 2. Being grounded for an entire summer is not too severe a punishment for wrecking part of a house.

_______ _______ 3. There is no way to politely decline to have your picture taken with someone you don't like.

_______ _______ 4. Making fun of someone's background is inexcusable behavior.

_______ _______ 5. Things that happened in the past have no effect on people today.

_______ _______ 6. Rarely are people exactly as they appear.

_______ _______ 7. Assuming a false identity in order to spy on others is despicable.

_______ _______ 8. If you reach a dead end, back up and try again.

_______ _______ 9. Never believe messages written by someone you have not met.

_______ _______ 10. Dedication and work are more important than heritage in achieving success in life.

_______ _______ 11. No major achievement is accomplished alone.

_______ _______ 12. Knowing how to use knowledge is more important than having a lot of knowledge.

HARRY POTTER AND THE GOBLET OF FIRE

by J. K. Rowling, Scholastic, 2002

Put a check on the line under AGREE if you agree with the statement. Put a check on the line under DISAGREE if you disagree with the statement.

AGREE   DISAGREE

_______   _______   1. An uneducated person finds it difficult to think for himself or herself.

_______   _______   2. There are many types of enslavement, and enslavement in any form is wrong.

_______   _______   3. Parents will make any sacrifice to keep their children from harm.

_______   _______   4. In a small community, each person's actions affect someone else.

_______   _______   5. Adolescents think far more about themselves than about others.

_______   _______   6. It is better to gather evidence slowly than to make snap judgments about people and situations.

_______   _______   7. A person's speech is the best indicator of his or her level of education.

_______   _______   8. A person unjustly accused of a crime will never be convicted.

_______   _______   9. Circumstantial evidence almost always points to the one guilty of a crime.

_______   _______   10. One person alone cannot change the rules of a society.

_______   _______   11. It is possible to be jealous of your best friend.

_______   _______   12. Fulfilling an obligation is more satisfying than following a personal desire.

HARRY POTTER AND THE ORDER OF THE PHOENIX
by J. K. Rowling, Scholastic, 2004

Put a check on the line under AGREE if you agree with the statement. Put a check on the line under DISAGREE if you disagree with the statement.

AGREE   DISAGREE

———   ———   1. People learn best through trial and error.

———   ———   2. Breaking a rule may have positive consequences.

———   ———   3. A group that does not work together for a just cause is destined for defeat.

———   ———   4. Segregation exists because groups do not make an effort to understand each other.

———   ———   5. Most students do not see the value of a good education.

———   ———   6. Telling a lie is often necessary for the good of others.

———   ———   7. Newspapers always print the truth.

———   ———   8. Withholding important information is the same as telling a lie.

———   ———   9. A good leader values loyalty above blind obedience.

———   ———   10. People are often promoted into jobs they cannot do, simply because they are good at a different job.

———   ———   11. Whispering campaigns are always filled with untruths and can destroy a person's reputation.

———   ———   12. Dreams can be upsetting even though they have no basis in fact.

HARRY POTTER AND THE PRISONER OF AZKABAN

by J. K. Rowling, Scholastic, 1999

Put a check on the line under AGREE if you agree with the statement. Put a check on the line under DISAGREE if you disagree with the statement.

AGREE   DISAGREE

——————   ——————   1. A bully always gets his or her way.

——————   ——————   2. Every situation has two sides, and both sides may be true.

——————   ——————   3. The legal system is more concerned with punishment than with justice.

——————   ——————   4. Friendship should have far greater value in a person's life than material gain.

——————   ——————   5. Few tasks are as easy to perform as they appear to be.

——————   ——————   6. You must always be polite to visiting relatives even if the relatives make unkind remarks about your loved ones.

——————   ——————   7. A hippogriff could exist only in a fantasy tale.

——————   ——————   8. When friends fall out, a crisis can bring them back together.

——————   ——————   9. Even the best of friends can become angry with each other.

——————   ——————   10. There may be very good reasons for one in authority to take away a treasured gift.

——————   ——————   11. False accusations are always made out of spite.

——————   ——————   12. Throughout history, good has always triumphed over evil.

HARRY POTTER AND THE SORCERER'S STONE

by J. K. Rowling, Scholastic, Arthur A. Levine Books, 1997

Put a check on the line under AGREE if you agree with the statement. Put a check on the line under DISAGREE if you disagree with the statement.

AGREE   DISAGREE

______   ______   1. When a visit from a relative is unwelcome, you don't have to be polite.

______   ______   2. An overindulged child expects to have all his or her wishes fulfilled.

______   ______   3. A monster temper tantrum usually gets results.

______   ______   4. When a stranger knocks on the door, you should expect exciting news.

______   ______   5. Going to a new school is usually a positive experience.

______   ______   6. Life in a new school can be miserable if you don't stick up for yourself.

______   ______   7. Not knowing the answers to a teacher's questions means you haven't done your homework.

______   ______   8. Arbitration is a peaceful way to settle an argument.

______   ______   9. An unfair punishment may be given when you won't tell on a friend.

______   ______   10. A referee in any team sport should show special favor to the underdogs.

______   ______   11. Everyone wants to live for ever.

______   ______   12. Love has the power to change lives.

HATCHET

by Gary Paulsen, Bradbury, 1987

Put a check on the line under AGREE if you agree with the statement. Put a check on the line under DISAGREE if you disagree with the statement.

AGREE   DISAGREE

_____   _____   1. Flying in a plane for the first time can be scary.

_____   _____   2. Divorce is sometimes necessary and unavoidable.

_____   _____   3. Often it is better not to know someone else's secret.

_____   _____   4. Anger can be a positive force in getting things done.

_____   _____   5. Patience is one of the most important things a human being can learn.

_____   _____   6. It is impossible for a city boy to survive alone in the wilderness.

_____   _____   7. Determination is more important than knowledge in wilderness survival.

_____   _____   8. It is possible to start a fire without matches.

_____   _____   9. Wild animals will always run from humans.

_____   _____   10. Change occurs in people when they successfully face difficult tasks.

_____   _____   11. Nature can be a friend or foe, but mostly it is a foe.

_____   _____   12. The most useful thing to have in the wilderness is a hatchet.

THE HAYMEADOW

by Gary Paulsen, Delacorte, 1992

Put a check on the line under AGREE if you agree with the statement. Put a check on the line under DISAGREE if you disagree with the statement.

AGREE   DISAGREE

———   ———   1. It is difficult to please a demanding father.

———   ———   2. Wishing can make things change.

———   ———   3. One should refuse a job that seems too big to handle.

———   ———   4. A boy should not be asked to take on a man's job.

———   ———   5. Sometimes it is necessary to shoot an animal.

———   ———   6. Some things in nature are not beautiful.

———   ———   7. Living alone can be very satisfying.

———   ———   8. Silence between two people can be comfortable.

———   ———   9. A less than perfect person can be admirable.

———   ———   10. When everything goes wrong, it's best to give up.

———   ———   11. Most people are capable of more than they believe they can do.

———   ———   12. Broken relationships can be mended.

HEIDI

by Johanna Spyri, Grosset & Dunlap, 1945

Put a check on the line under AGREE if you agree with the statement. Put a check on the line under DISAGREE if you disagree with the statement.

AGREE   DISAGREE

——————   ——————   1. It is not necessary to go to school to learn.

——————   ——————   2. A child raised in the country will be unhappy in the city.

——————   ——————   3. Rules are necessary in a civilized society.

——————   ——————   4. A sense of humor can lighten a difficult situation.

——————   ——————   5. Keeping busy put an end to homesickness.

——————   ——————   6. It is not always easy to tell fact from fiction.

——————   ——————   7. Keeping unhappiness bottled up inside is dangerous.

——————   ——————   8. The best way to handle disappointment is to smile.

——————   ——————   9. Jealousy can destroy a relationship.

——————   ——————   10. Brave acts can be carried out by people who are afraid.

——————   ——————   11. Good health and a positive attitude go together.

——————   ——————   12. Old people never change their ways.

THE HERO AND THE CROWN

by Robin McKinley, Greenwillow Books, 1984

Put a check on the line under AGREE if you agree with the statement. Put a check on the line under DISAGREE if you disagree with the statement.

AGREE   DISAGREE

______   ______   1. To achieve expertise in any area, an apprenticeship is necessary.

______   ______   2. In fantasy tales, all dragon slayers are male.

______   ______   3. The daughter of a king should expect to have many enemies.

______   ______   4. One should never eat a strange plant at the urging of others.

______   ______   5. Love and care can bring a hopelessly sick animal back to health.

______   ______   6. One who enters a bonfire cannot escape unharmed.

______   ______   7. A crown brings great power to its owner.

______   ______   8. The power of evil can destroy the innocent.

______   ______   9. In every fantasy tale, the hero or heroine must undertake a difficult and dangerous mission.

______   ______   10. In every fantasy tale, good triumphs over evil.

______   ______   11. Once a reputation is acquired, it cannot be dispelled.

______   ______   12. Having too much self-confidence is as bad as having too little.

HIDE AND SEEK

by Ida Vos, Scholastic, 1981

Put a check on the line under AGREE if you agree with the statement. Put a check on the line under DISAGREE if you disagree with the statement.

AGREE   DISAGREE

_____   _____   1. You cannot wipe out a religion by persecuting the people who practice it.

_____   _____   2. Prejudice toward another group of people is learned from one's parents and is usually passed on to one's children.

_____   _____   3. In wartime, noncombatants suffer as much as or more than soldiers.

_____   _____   4. There are many good reasons why parents would leave their children in a stranger's care.

_____   _____   5. Stealing food for your hungry family should not be considered a crime.

_____   _____   6. The segregation of any one group of people from a community is a thing of the past in the United States.

_____   _____   7. Risking your life to help a stranger, even if you know his or her cause is just, is foolish.

_____   _____   8. Perpetuating a lie is not wrong if the purpose is to save lives.

_____   _____   9. In wartime, many children must accept responsibilities beyond their years.

_____   _____   10. Most people will commit acts against others while part of a group that they would never commit alone.

_____   _____   11. Families torn apart by war can never be put back together again and function in the same way as before.

_____   _____   12. Many things that are important before a war become trivial after the war.

THE HOBBIT

by J.R.R. Tolkien, Houghton Mifflin, 1984

Put a check on the line under AGREE if you agree with the statement. Put a check on the line under DISAGREE if you disagree with the statement.

AGREE   DISAGREE

_______   _______   1. When unexpected company arrives, pretend you are not home.

_______   _______   2. People are often expected to do jobs for which they are not trained.

_______   _______   3. A letter that could be read only at night would be found only in a fantasy tale.

_______   _______   4. The most desirable power of a magic ring would be to give good health to the owner.

_______   _______   5. Every person has more ability than he thinks he or she has.

_______   _______   6. Only a greedy person ignores those in need.

_______   _______   7. It is possible for an enemy to become a friend.

_______   _______   8. Good always triumphs over evil.

_______   _______   9. You should never turn your back on one who has done you a good deed.

_______   _______   10. A good deed can be mistaken for treachery.

_______   _______   11. Great riches are not nearly as important as friendship.

_______   _______   12. Returning to a quiet home after a great adventure is always satisfying.

HOLES

by Louis Sachar, Farrar, Straus & Giroux, 1998

Put a check on the line under AGREE if you agree with the statement. Put a check on the line under DISAGREE if you disagree with the statement.

AGREE   DISAGREE

______   ______   1. Jails are filled with people unjustly accused of crimes.

______   ______   2. A whole town might turn on a person believed to be a criminal.

______   ______   3. The inability to read and write can lead to a life of crime.

______   ______   4. The purpose of a juvenile detention camp is to make good citizens of offenders.

______   ______   5. Believing that bad luck is your fate is the same as giving up.

______   ______   6. A person who enjoys being cruel to others is mentally ill.

______   ______   7. The most important things to take on a desert journey are matches.

______   ______   8. Some prisons have no need for guards or fences.

______   ______   9. Only superstitious people would believe in a gypsy curse.

______   ______   10. At times, blackmail may be justified.

______   ______   11. There is more than one kind of courage.

______   ______   12. Most people have ulterior motives for the things they do.

HOMECOMING

by Cynthia Voight, Atheneum, 1981

Put a check on the line under AGREE if you agree with the statement. Put a check on the line under DISAGREE if you disagree with the statement.

AGREE   DISAGREE

_______   _______   1. People may be limited in what they say and do by the expectations of others.

_______   _______   2. In most people, a sense of duty triumphs over personal wishes.

_______   _______   3. A person bound by habit will not grow mentally.

_______   _______   4. The conventions of any society exist for very good reasons.

_______   _______   5. Home is not a place; it is family members who care about each other.

_______   _______   6. The more flexible a person is, the better he or she will adapt to new situations.

_______   _______   7. It is possible for a parent to have very good reasons to abandon his or her children.

_______   _______   8. The best way to react to a threat is to close yourself off from others.

_______   _______   9. Money equals power and control.

_______   _______   10. Stealing food is not wrong if you are hungry and have no money.

_______   _______   11. Never trust or accept any kind of help from a stranger.

_______   _______   12. Freedom and independence are states that most people desire but few people achieve.

HOMER PRICE

by Robert McCloskey, Viking, 1943

Put a check on the line under AGREE if you agree with the statement. Put a check on the line under DISAGREE if you disagree with the statement.

AGREE   DISAGREE

_____   _____   1. Some laborsaving devices cause more work, not less.

_____   _____   2. It is good to take time off from work to play.

_____   _____   3. People who use machines without reading the instructions are asking for trouble.

_____   _____   4. People in the 1940s lived life at a slower pace than people today.

_____   _____   5. It is possible to create a demand for an item that hasn't been selling.

_____   _____   6. "The world will beat a path to the door of the man who invents a better mousetrap."

_____   _____   7. Not all superheroes are admirable.

_____   _____   8. Building a subdivision causes the destruction of wildlife.

_____   _____   9. Without advertising, businesses would have to close their doors.

_____   _____   10. Children of the 1940s had more vivid imaginations than children today, because they did not grow up with television.

_____   _____   11. One should never accept a reward for doing the right thing.

_____   _____   12. Some problems can be solved only with the help of friends.

HOMESICK: MY OWN STORY

by Jean Fritz, Putnam's, 1992

Put a check on the line under AGREE if you agree with the statement. Put a check on the line under DISAGREE if you disagree with the statement.

AGREE   DISAGREE

______   ______   1. One can be born in another country yet be an American citizen.

______   ______   2. It is impossible to love a country if you are despised there as a foreigner.

______   ______   3. It is possible to be homesick for a country in which you have never lived.

______   ______   4. Missionaries risk their lives daily to work in foreign lands.

______   ______   5. One can become used to being constantly insulted and not let the insults hurt.

______   ______   6. A revolution in a country is the result of poor treatment of the people by the government.

______   ______   7. Home schooling is as effective as attending a public school.

______   ______   8. Fear is a good thing if it leads to positive action.

______   ______   9. It is not rude to refuse to sing another country's national anthem.

______   ______   10. A child who has a servant to look after her will never learn to do anything for herself.

______   ______   11. To be raised in one country, yet to be a citizen of another, would be very confusing for a child.

______   ______   12. Every American should see his or her country through the eyes of one who has never seen it.

HOPE WAS HERE

by Joan Bauer, Putnam's, 2000

Put a check on the line under AGREE if you agree with the statement. Put a check on the line under DISAGREE if you disagree with the statement.

AGREE   DISAGREE

______   ______   1. A mother might have a good reason for abandoning her baby.

______   ______   2. Moving to a new town is always difficult, even if the move seems to be for the better.

______   ______   3. Names can give meaning to our lives.

______   ______   4. Making a positive difference in the lives of others should be every person's goal.

______   ______   5. Changes of any kind help one to look at life differently.

______   ______   6. The only thing certain in life is change; those who refuse to adapt will be left behind.

______   ______   7. Even when you are not in school, life is a test.

______   ______   8. Facing disappointment makes a person stronger.

______   ______   9. Every member of a community has an obligation to make it a better place to live.

______   ______   10. Our hopes are not always realized in the way we imagine.

______   ______   11. It is important to accept people as they are, not as we wish them to be.

______   ______   12. A true father is there for his kid every single day.

THE HOUSE OF DIES DREAR

by Virginia Hamilton, Macmillan, 1968

Put a check on the line under AGREE if you agree with the statement. Put a check on the line under DISAGREE if you disagree with the statement.

AGREE   DISAGREE

_______   _______   1. Moving to a new home in a new community offers added opportunities for success.

_______   _______   2. People are often wrongly judged by their appearance.

_______   _______   3. Ghost legends are attached to many old homes.

_______   _______   4. Asking too many questions can irritate your parents.

_______   _______   5. Older children should not be expected to look after their younger brothers and sisters.

_______   _______   6. When strange children make fun of you, ignore them.

_______   _______   7. It is not a good idea to rely on first impressions.

_______   _______   8. You know someone is telling the truth if that person looks you right in the eye.

_______   _______   9. There is something very wrong with a town that does not welcome newcomers.

_______   _______   10. When townsfolk shun one particular family, there must be a very good reason.

_______   _______   11. When a poor man won t touch a treasure, he must be afraid of going to jail for stealing.

_______   _______   12. A family of rascals would be fun next-door neighbors.

HOW TO EAT FRIED WORMS

by Thomas Rockwell, Franklin Watts, 1973

Put a check on the line under AGREE if you agree with the statement. Put a check on the line under DISAGREE if you disagree with the statement.

AGREE   DISAGREE

_______   _______   1. Eating worms can make you sick, because worms are poisonous.

_______   _______   2. A bet can end a long friendship.

_______   _______   3. Taking peaches off a tree without permission is stealing.

_______   _______   4. A stubborn person may be his or her own worst enemy.

_______   _______   5. Waking your parents in the middle of the night is not a good idea.

_______   _______   6. You should forgive a friend who lets you down.

_______   _______   7. Cheating to win a bet is sometimes okay.

_______   _______   8. Being alone at night is scary.

_______   _______   9. An apology is worthless if it is not sincere.

_______   _______   10. Some punishments are well deserved.

_______   _______   11. It is not always easy to apologize.

_______   _______   12. You can do anything you set your mind to.

HUMBUG

by Nina Bawden, Houghton Mifflin, 1992

Put a check on the line under AGREE if you agree with the statement. Put a check on the line under DISAGREE if you disagree with the statement.

AGREE   DISAGREE

______   ______   1. Being placed in a home with strangers, even for a short time, may be upsetting and frightening.

______   ______   2. An outspoken child is an unmanageable child.

______   ______   3. Senior citizens contribute nothing to a household and should be ignored.

______   ______   4. Refusing to accept the truth causes more harm than good.

______   ______   5. Arrogance can get a person into trouble.

______   ______   6. Elderly people prefer to live in the comfort of their children's homes.

______   ______   7. Some people live lives of pretense and deception because they have never achieved success on their own.

______   ______   8. When adults won t believe you are innocent of a crime, the best thing for you to do is run away.

______   ______   9. It is impossible for a child to disprove a false accusation.

______   ______   10. Spitefulness never brings satisfaction to the perpetrator.

______   ______   11. Everyone needs a quiet place to escape to now and then.

______   ______   12. Wickedness may wear a mask of kindness.

THE HUNDRED DRESSES

by Eleanor Estes, Harcourt, 1972

Put a check on the line under AGREE if you agree with the statement. Put a check
on the line under DISAGREE if you disagree with the statement.

AGREE   DISAGREE

_______   _______   1. Only a poor reader does not like to read out loud
in class.

_______   _______   2. Teasing someone can be either affectionate or
cruel.

_______   _______   3. People tend to shun those who are different.

_______   _______   4. A person who is afraid to laugh does not want to
be noticed.

_______   _______   5. Not speaking up to right a wrong is as bad as
doing the wrong.

_______   _______   6. Children daydream to escape an unhappy life.

_______   _______   7. Some people will do anything to be part of a
group.

_______   _______   8. If you are the target of teasing, it is your own
fault for not standing up for yourself.

_______   _______   9. A bright blue day may turn dull when there is no
friend to share it with.

_______   _______   10. Children who reject those who are different are
not aware that they are being cruel.

_______   _______   11. Standing up for what you believe is right can
make you lose friends.

_______   _______   12. Feeling ashamed of yourself should lead to the
righting of a wrong.

I SAILED WITH COLUMBUS

by Miriam Schlein, HarperCollins, 1991

Put a check on the line under AGREE if you agree with the statement. Put a check on the line under DISAGREE if you disagree with the statement.

AGREE   DISAGREE

1. A boy raised in a monastery would live a very quiet, sheltered life.

2. A new adventure can be exciting and frightening at the same time.

3. People will work harder if they are offered a reward.

4. The problem with telling a lie is that you always get caught.

5. It is okay for hungry people to steal food.

6. It is always possible to communicate with one who speaks a different language.

7. Never eat a food if you do not know what it is.

8. Time goes by slowly for lazy people.

9. A friend can be a great comfort when rough sailing sets in.

10. A good leader can inspire faith even when the situation is discouraging.

11. A cherished object can be recovered; a lost reputation can never be.

12. It is possible to feel happy and sad at the same time.

IDA EARLY COMES OVER THE MOUNTAIN

by Robert Burch, Avon Books, 1980

Put a check on the line under AGREE if you agree with the statement. Put a check on the line under DISAGREE if you disagree with the statement.

AGREE   DISAGREE

______   ______   1. One who has accepted a heavy responsibility does not welcome another person wanting to take over.

______   ______   2. Exaggeration is the same as lying.

______   ______   3. Unconventional people have more fun in life than conventional people do.

______   ______   4. It is never acceptable to make fun of someone's appearance.

______   ______   5. Only insecure people make up stories about who they are and where they have been.

______   ______   6. Being part of a peer group is more important than standing up for what you know is right.

______   ______   7. A person can be needed and not wanted at the same time.

______   ______   8. In the Depression years, everyone was poor.

______   ______   9. A person who cannot prove what he or she says should never be believed.

______   ______   10. Lazy people are good at getting others to do their work.

______   ______   11. Never allow a stranger to enter your house.

______   ______   12. Only the very weak will refuse to stick up for a friend.

THE ILLYRIAN ADVENTURE

by Lloyd Alexander, E. P. Dutton, 1986

Put a check on the line under AGREE if you agree with the statement. Put a check on the line under DISAGREE if you disagree with the statement.

AGREE   DISAGREE

_______   _______   1. Searching for a lost treasure is an exciting adventure.

_______   _______   2. A young person and an old person can be very good friends.

_______   _______   3. The most valuable thing a person has is his or her reputation.

_______   _______   4. Honor is as important as justice.

_______   _______   5. Oppressed people should rebel against their ruler.

_______   _______   6. Hiring a stranger as a guide is foolish.

_______   _______   7. A village storyteller is a historian.

_______   _______   8. Being arrested for no reason is frightening.

_______   _______   9. When two sides can't agree, they must compromise.

_______   _______   10. The best way to hide something is to put it in plain sight.

_______   _______   11. It is foolish to risk your life for another.

_______   _______   12. A determined mind means success.

IN THE SHADOW OF THE PALI

by Lisa Cindrich, Putnam's, 2002

Put a check on the line under AGREE if you agree with the statement. Put a check on the line under DISAGREE if you disagree with the statement.

AGREE   DISAGREE

_______   _______   1. People are naturally interested in the strange or unusual.

_______   _______   2. People are helpless against nature.

_______   _______   3. All human beings have a desire to succeed in whatever they try.

_______   _______   4. In the 1860s, lepers in Hawaii were abandoned on a barren island.

_______   _______   5. A tall mountain can be beautiful and frightening at the same time.

_______   _______   6. Starving human beings quickly become uncivilized.

_______   _______   7. There are places in the world today where there are no laws.

_______   _______   8. When challenged by a stronger enemy, it is wisest to give in.

_______   _______   9. Missionaries all over the world risk their lives to help people they don't know.

_______   _______   10. People throughout history have paid with their lives for their beliefs.

_______   _______   11. Surviving alone on an island with little food and shelter is impossible.

_______   _______   12. Kind people may become cruel when their basic needs are not met.

THE INCREDIBLE JOURNEY

by *Sheila Burnford,* Little, Brown, 1961

Put a check on the line under AGREE if you agree with the statement. Put a check on the line under DISAGREE if you disagree with the statement.

AGREE   DISAGREE

——————   ——————   1. If a person reads only half of a note, he or she may take the wrong action.

——————   ——————   2. The young can benefit from the wisdom of the old if they take time to listen.

——————   ——————   3. If something is incredible, that means it can't happen.

——————   ——————   4. A misunderstanding can occur when directions are unclear.

——————   ——————   5. There are good reasons why a person might shoot a dog.

——————   ——————   6. Unlikely companions complement each other when there is a job to be done.

——————   ——————   7. Caring for another's pets for pay is more trouble than it is worth.

——————   ——————   8. A man who feeds animals at his kitchen table is asking for trouble.

——————   ——————   9. Dogs and cats can never exist peacefully together.

——————   ——————   10. The biggest challenge to be faced in the wilderness is wild animals.

——————   ——————   11. Even the most responsible person may lose a pet.

——————   ——————   12. A dog or cat can find its way home over great distances by instinct.

THE INDIAN IN THE CUPBOARD

by Lynne Reid Banks, Doubleday, 1980

Put a check on the line under AGREE if you agree with the statement. Put a check on the line under DISAGREE if you disagree with the statement.

AGREE   DISAGREE

_______   _______   1. Even if a birthday present seems to have no use, you should thank the giver politely.

_______   _______   2. The demands of a new friend are easy to meet until they become too numerous.

_______   _______   3. When something totally out of the ordinary happens, you should immediately tell your parents.

_______   _______   4. It is easy to make mistakes when you don't have all the facts.

_______   _______   5. People often do things they don't want to do.

_______   _______   6. Dreams can seem so real that you believe them.

_______   _______   7. It's hard to walk in someone else's shoes.

_______   _______   8. Big brothers are good for only one thing, bossing you around.

_______   _______   9. Trying to keep a secret is a lot like trying to keep a pot from boiling over.

_______   _______   10. Best friends can be a pain when they get too nosy.

_______   _______   11. It is hard to keep a good reputation if you run with rascals.

_______   _______   12. People should not always believe what they see.

INKHEART

by Cornelia Funke, The Chicken House, 2003

Put a check on the line under AGREE if you agree with the statement. Put a check on the line under DISAGREE if you disagree with the statement.

AGREE   DISAGREE

_____   _____   1. There may be good reasons why a parent refuses to read aloud to a child.

_____   _____   2. It is a fortunate child who grows up surrounded by books.

_____   _____   3. It is possible for characters to step out of books into real life.

_____   _____   4. Some people purposefully keep their talents hidden.

_____   _____   5. Every fantasy tale includes an evil character who will eventually be defeated.

_____   _____   6. It is impossible to hide from evil in the world.

_____   _____   7. A person who is cruel to animals will be equally cruel to people.

_____   _____   8. If a warning of danger is given without proof, it is best to ignore it.

_____   _____   9. It is possible to be loyal to two people with opposing views.

_____   _____   10. It is often necessary for a parent to keep secrets from his or her children.

_____   _____   11. Solutions to many of life's problems can be found in books.

_____   _____   12. There is never a good reason to destroy books.

THE IRON GIANT

by Ted Hughes, Faber & Faber, 1985

Put a check on the line under AGREE if you agree with the statement. Put a check on the line under DISAGREE if you disagree with the statement.

AGREE   DISAGREE

_____   _____   1. Many small communities do not welcome strangers.

_____   _____   2. Many people who appear to be frightening are gentle people in reality.

_____   _____   3. Peaceful solutions to problems work better than violence.

_____   _____   4. Humans regard creatures from space as something found only in science-fiction stories.

_____   _____   5. People fear what they do not understand.

_____   _____   6. If every nation were well armed with the latest weapons, there would be no wars.

_____   _____   7. A voracious appetite can lead to obesity.

_____   _____   8. The only way to banish shame is to make amends.

_____   _____   9. When people who have rejected you ask for help, you should refuse to give it.

_____   _____   10. There are monstrous things in space that can destroy the Earth.

_____   _____   11. Keeping your distance in the face of danger is cowardly.

_____   _____   12. Only an unhappy person has every demand instantly satisfied.

ISLAND OF THE BLUE DOLPHINS

by Scott O'Dell, Houghton Mifflin, 1960

Put a check on the line under AGREE if you agree with the statement. Put a check on the line under DISAGREE if you disagree with the statement.

AGREE   DISAGREE

_______   _______   1. It is possible for a bad enemy to become a good friend.

_______   _______   2. It is often difficult to get along with people from another country.

_______   _______   3. Warriors who fight in battle must believe in their cause.

_______   _______   4. Most family members will risk their lives for other family members.

_______   _______   5. A girl raised in an island tribe can survive alone on an island.

_______   _______   6. The best way to get rid of wild dogs is to hide from them.

_______   _______   7. A wild dog is born wild. It does not become vicious later in life.

_______   _______   8. Exploring a cave alone is a foolish thing to do.

_______   _______   9. The two most important things a human being needs to survive are food and fire.

_______   _______   10. To be rescued when you have survived alone on an island is not always welcome.

_______   _______   11. An entire group of people displaced from their homes will never be happy anywhere else.

_______   _______   12. Nations have always fought with each other and will continue to fight with each other.

JACOB HAVE I LOVED

by Katherine Paterson, Crowell, 1980

Put a check on the line under AGREE if you agree with the statement. Put a check on the line under DISAGREE if you disagree with the statement.

AGREE   DISAGREE

_____   _____   1. Judging a person by his or her appearance is unreliable.

_____   _____   2. Marching to a different drummer can be very painful.

_____   _____   3. In a disaster, people look after themselves and ignore others in need.

_____   _____   4. Sibling rivalry is natural and to be expected.

_____   _____   5. In many families, one child gets all the attention.

_____   _____   6. Having no dreams for the future is the same as having no desire to succeed.

_____   _____   7. War between people or countries is never justified.

_____   _____   8. Writing poetry for a living can lead to poverty.

_____   _____   9. Every person needs at least one good friend.

_____   _____   10. Anger can be self-defeating.

_____   _____   11. Holding on to a dream is important.

_____   _____   12. Old differences can be resolved if all parties are willing.

JAMES AND THE GIANT PEACH

by Roald Dahl, Alfred A. Knopf, 1961

Put a check on the line under AGREE if you agree with the statement. Put a check on the line under DISAGREE if you disagree with the statement.

AGREE   DISAGREE

_____   _____   1. Anyone forced to live with wicked relatives should run away.

_____   _____   2. Doing all the work around the house can be rewarding.

_____   _____   3. If there were magic crystals to make everyone happy, there would be no more wars.

_____   _____   4. A dormant tree can never produce fruit.

_____   _____   5. Fear of the dark is an unreasonable fear.

_____   _____   6. Finding a light at the end of a tunnel means that a problem has been solved.

_____   _____   7. Losing something valuable is not always a bad thing.

_____   _____   8. Earthworms are very useful creatures.

_____   _____   9. It is possible for a peach to grow to the size of a house.

_____   _____   10. The air may be filled with many flying objects other than birds.

_____   _____   11. Discovering how an insect grows can be fascinating.

_____   _____   12. A peach could roll down the street only in a fantasy tale.

JASON'S GOLD

by Will Hobbs, William Morrow, 1999

Put a check on the line under AGREE if you agree with the statement. Put a check on the line under DISAGREE if you disagree with the statement.

AGREE   DISAGREE

1. Elderly people have experiences to share that can be very useful for the young.

2. Being a stowaway on a ship doesn't harm anyone, especially if it is the only way you can get to your destination.

3. Getting to the Alaskan goldfields took far more know-how and courage than getting to the Californian goldfields.

4. A greedy captain, in overloading his ship, is risking immediate income for long-term gain.

5. People who are nice to you when they don't have to be must have ulterior motives.

6. Jack London, a character in this novel, was a real person.

7. As there were no health inspectors in the nineteenth century, it was risky to eat any food not prepared at home.

8. It is impossible to travel in Alaska by boat in winter, because the lakes and streams freeze over.

9. Moose like people and make good pets.

10. The only cure for an infected limb in the nineteenth century was its removal.

11. Flash floods are a constant danger wherever you find streams.

12. Traveling long distances alone is better than having a companion, because you can move at your own pace.

JERICHO'S JOURNEY

by G. Clifton Wisler, Puffin Books, 1995,

Put a check on the line under AGREE if you agree with the statement. Put a check on the line under DISAGREE if you disagree with the statement.

AGREE   DISAGREE

_____   _____   1. Moving to an unknown land from a comfortable home is foolish.

_____   _____   2. Never take a ne er-do-well on a long journey.

_____   _____   3. Exaggerating is the same as telling lies.

_____   _____   4. A starving person would eat a rat.

_____   _____   5. Never ford a river if you don't know how to swim.

_____   _____   6. The best place to be in a thunderstorm is under a tree.

_____   _____   7. When religious beliefs conflict with travel plans, put the religious beliefs first.

_____   _____   8. Taking a bath in a cold spring will make you ill.

_____   _____   9. Never trust a stranger.

_____   _____   10. Surviving hard times makes a person stronger in meeting new challenges.

_____   _____   11. Being a leader is far more difficult than being a follower.

_____   _____   12. Sleeping in a real bed after months of sleeping on the ground can be uncomfortable.

JIM UGLY

by Sid Fleischman, Greenwillow Books, 1992

Put a check on the line under AGREE if you agree with the statement. Put a check on the line under DISAGREE if you disagree with the statement.

AGREE   DISAGREE

______   ______   1. The Wild West was not as wild as the movies would have you think.

______   ______   2. Some dogs will respond only to their masters.

______   ______   3. Stealing something of value is okay if it will keep innocent people from being swindled.

______   ______   4. Telling a lie is permissible if its purpose is to save a life.

______   ______   5. Bounty hunters in the Old West were criminals rather than lawmen.

______   ______   6. A dog can't be fooled about the death of its master.

______   ______   7. Taking another's place is okay on stage but not in real life.

______   ______   8. It is natural for a child to defend a parent accused of a crime.

______   ______   9. Some parents leave their children because they have to, not because they want to.

______   ______   10. Salting a mine is an unscrupulous activity.

______   ______   11. There is no relationship stronger than that between a boy and a dog.

______   ______   12. Welcoming a stranger into your family without asking questions is a foolish thing to do.

JOHNNY TREMAIN

by Esther Forbes, Houghton Mifflin, 1943

Put a check on the line under AGREE if you agree with the statement. Put a check on the line under DISAGREE if you disagree with the statement.

AGREE   DISAGREE

———   ———   1. Having a good opinion of oneself is desirable.

———   ———   2. One who breaks rules on purpose is asking for trouble.

———   ———   3. Only an evil person would deliberately injure another.

———   ———   4. Some people are too proud to accept honest work.

———   ———   5. Arrogance can get a person into trouble.

———   ———   6. It is impossible to ask for help from those you have mocked.

———   ———   7. Destroying another's property is sometimes necessary.

———   ———   8. People who pay taxes should be able to vote for or against the taxes.

———   ———   9. Ignoring a deadline can lead to problems.

———   ———   10. Fighting is the only solution when both sides believe they are right.

———   ———   11. Doing one's duty is not always easy.

———   ———   12. An untrained army fighting against professional troops will lose.

JOURNEY

by Patricia MacLachlan, Yearling Books, 1993

Put a check on the line under AGREE if you agree with the statement. Put a check on the line under DISAGREE if you disagree with the statement.

AGREE   DISAGREE

_____   _____   1. There may be good reasons why a mother abandons her children.

_____   _____   2. A family involves more than having two parents in the home.

_____   _____   3. A camera can tell the past, present, and future.

_____   _____   4. Refusing to accept the truth is a good way to deal with adversity.

_____   _____   5. If things are too difficult to accept, you should deny that they exist.

_____   _____   6. Two people can look at the same picture and see different things.

_____   _____   7. Two people can react very differently to the same set of circumstances.

_____   _____   8. Some people believe only what they want to believe.

_____   _____   9. Family life has changed drastically in the United States in the last 30 years.

_____   _____   10. Lonely people often find companionship in a pet.

_____   _____   11. Grandparents should not be expected to raise their grandchildren; they have already raised one family.

_____   _____   12. A person cannot be taken advantage of if he or she does not want to be.

JOURNEY HOME

by Yoshiko Uchida, Atheneum, 1978

Put a check on the line under AGREE if you agree with the statement. Put a check on the line under DISAGREE if you disagree with the statement.

AGREE   DISAGREE

______   ______   1. It is possible for law-abiding citizens to be locked up.

______   ______   2. War creates an atmosphere of fear and distrust.

______   ______   3. A concentration camp is a place for criminals.

______   ______   4. Treasured objects have a life of their own.

______   ______   5. It is possible to leave a bit of yourself with a friend.

______   ______   6. Shy people only seem to be unfriendly.

______   ______   7. "Nothing ever stays the same" is a rule of nature.

______   ______   8. When a burden is too heavy to carry, ask for help.

______   ______   9. Sometimes it is difficult to forgive yourself.

______   ______   10. Harboring resentment can lead to a life of unhappiness.

______   ______   11. Prejudice is learned from older people.

______   ______   12. Achieving a dream does not always bring happiness.

JOURNEY TO JO'BURG

by Beverly Naidoo, Lippincott, 1985

Put a check on the line under AGREE if you agree with the statement. Put a check on the line under DISAGREE if you disagree with the statement.

AGREE   DISAGREE

———   ———   1. Children should not make a long journey alone.

———   ———   2. Going on a trip with no food or money is foolish.

———   ———   3. Poor people often do not seek medical help.

———   ———   4. A starving person should not be punished for taking an orange off a tree.

———   ———   5. Being in a big city for the first time is exciting.

———   ———   6. When a kind stranger offers help, take it.

———   ———   7. One should never take advice from strangers.

———   ———   8. Spending the night in a strange house is scary.

———   ———   9. Prejudice is learned at home.

———   ———   10. When employers are unfair, workers should strike.

———   ———   11. Waiting is difficult when you are holding a sick child.

———   ———   12. People who have no power suffer many injustices.

JULIE OF THE WOLVES

by Jean Craighead George, HarperCollins, 1972

Put a check on the line under AGREE if you agree with the statement. Put a check on the line under DISAGREE if you disagree with the statement.

AGREE   DISAGREE

_______   _______   1. All civilizations must adapt to change or die.

_______   _______   2. A thirteen-year-old girl is not old enough to make decisions about her life.

_______   _______   3. It is foolish to carry on a steady correspondence with someone you have never met.

_______   _______   4. Most people tell you only what they think you want to hear.

_______   _______   5. Wolves and humans are natural enemies.

_______   _______   6. It is possible for a human to communicate with a wolf.

_______   _______   7. Living with people is preferable by far to living with a pack of wolves.

_______   _______   8. Bounty hunters make their living killing wild animals.

_______   _______   9. It is not possible to survive alone on the Alaskan tundra.

_______   _______   10. Many people refuse to accept that the past is gone.

_______   _______   11. While cultures must change, their traditions may remain the same.

_______   _______   12. It is extremely difficult to choose between opposites.

KEEPER OF THE DOVES

by Betsy Byars, Viking, 2002

Put a check on the line under AGREE if you agree with the statement. Put a check on the line under DISAGREE if you disagree with the statement.

AGREE   DISAGREE

————   ————   1. Words can both hurt and heal.

————   ————   2. A mother who spends all her time in her room has, in effect, abandoned her children.

————   ————   3. Writing poetry can help make sense of the world.

————   ————   4. Children in the same family have similar personalities.

————   ————   5. All fathers wish to have a son.

————   ————   6. Some children delight in terrifying others with scary stories and cruel games.

————   ————   7. Terrible stories are often made up about people who live alone.

————   ————   8. Poets are usually accused of wasting time and not wanting to get a real job.

————   ————   9. Being a member of a wealthy family means you have the freedom to do whatever you desire.

————   ————   10. "As long as there are words, nobody need ever die."

————   ————   11. The pictures you take with a camera reveal a lot about you.

————   ————   12. Children in the early twentieth century had far less freedom than children today.

KIDNAPPING KEVIN KOWALSKI

by Mary Jane Auch, Holiday House, 1990

Put a check on the line under AGREE if you agree with the statement. Put a check on the line under DISAGREE if you disagree with the statement.

AGREE   **DISAGREE**

______   ______   1. In any group of friends there will be one who is cautious, one who is adventurous, and one who is nutty.

______   ______   2. You should expect a person to be very different after a serious accident.

______   ______   3. It is natural for a mother to overprotect a child who has been injured in an accident.

______   ______   4. Everyone is capable of doing more than he or she believes is possible.

______   ______   5. The only thing that keeps one from achieving a goal is a lack of confidence.

______   ______   6. Fathers expect more from their sons than mothers do.

______   ______   7. Some parents don't care where their children are or what they do.

______   ______   8. Learning to live with a disability is one of the most difficult tasks a person must perform.

______   ______   9. Telling a lie is okay if it is will help another person.

______   ______   10. A true friend would not ask you to do something risky.

______   ______   11. True friendship can withstand drastic changes.

______   ______   12. Deceiving one's parents as to where you are is never the right thing to do.

KINDERTRANSPORT

by Olga Levy Drucker, Henry Holt, 1992

Put a check on the line under AGREE if you agree with the statement. Put a check on the line under DISAGREE if you disagree with the statement.

AGREE   DISAGREE

_____   _____   1. Only uncaring parents would send a child away from home.

_____   _____   2. Throughout history, people have suffered greatly because of their religion.

_____   _____   3. Moving to a new city without your family is a frightening experience.

_____   _____   4. War changes the lives of both soldiers and civilians.

_____   _____   5. Loud voices and heavy footsteps in the night mean trouble.

_____   _____   6. It is impossible to learn a new language in a short time.

_____   _____   7. Children who move around a lot are smarter than those who never travel.

_____   _____   8. In World War II, more civilians than soldiers lost their lives.

_____   _____   9. A new house can connect with every sense in your body.

_____   _____   10. New students in a school are usually given a hard time by other students.

_____   _____   11. Air raids are a part of daily life in wartime.

_____   _____   12. People learn prejudice toward others from their parents.

KING OF THE WIND

by Marguerite Henry, Rand McNally, 1976

Put a check on the line under AGREE if you agree with the statement. Put a check on the line under DISAGREE if you disagree with the statement.

AGREE   DISAGREE

————   ————   1. Taking care of an animal can be a privilege.

————   ————   2. Dreams can give you direction for your life.

————   ————   3. A person who is cruel to animals has no conscience.

————   ————   4. One who starves horses to save money should be put in jail.

————   ————   5. Keeping a promise is very difficult to do at times.

————   ————   6. Days can often seem like years when something important is going to happen.

————   ————   7. Defending an animal you love may lead to a serious injury.

————   ————   8. A young horse, like a person, can show promise that is never realized.

————   ————   9. Horses play a far less important role today than two hundred years ago.

————   ————   10. Some people see the greatness in a horse that others miss.

————   ————   11. Only human beings demonstrate the trait of loyalty.

————   ————   12. Disappointment is a part of life and should be expected.

KIRA-KIRA

by Cynthia Kadohata, Atheneum, 2004

Put a check on the line under AGREE if you agree with the statement. Put a check on the line under DISAGREE if you disagree with the statement.

AGREE   DISAGREE

______   ______   1. Many people don't trust banks, with good reason.

______   ______   2. It is often difficult to be a good loser.

______   ______   3. Ignorance is a major cause of prejudice.

______   ______   4. Too many people in a small space may lead to conflict.

______   ______   5. Classmates ignore a new student because they have been taught to beware of strangers.

______   ______   6. There are often good reasons why one child in a family receives more attention than the other children.

______   ______   7. It is natural for sisters to be jealous of each other.

______   ______   8. It is wrong for family members to keep secrets from one another.

______   ______   9. Parents who work long hours choose to do so.

______   ______   10. Shoplifting is a serious offense, usually leading to even more serious crimes.

______   ______   11. The truth should be told, even when telling a lie is easier.

______   ______   12. A life without dreams holds out no hope for the future.

KNEEKNOCK RISE

by Natalie Babbitt, Farrar, Straus & Giroux, 1970

Put a check on the line under AGREE if you agree with the statement. Put a check on the line under DISAGREE if you disagree with the statement.

AGREE   DISAGREE

———   ———   1. Only foolish people spread rumors.

———   ———   2. It is possible to dislike someone you have only just met.

———   ———   3. When a pet becomes very old, it should be put to sleep.

———   ———   4. Knowledge and wisdom are not the same thing.

———   ———   5. Accepting a dare is a foolish thing to do.

———   ———   6. Boys are always braver than girls.

———   ———   7. The greatest fear is fear of the unknown.

———   ———   8. Some people refuse to believe the truth.

———   ———   9. A good-luck charm may bring good luck.

———   ———   10. Superstition has no basis in fact.

———   ———   11. Strange mountain creatures do exist.

———   ———   12. A person cannot be brave if he or she is afraid.

KNIGHTS OF THE KITCHEN TABLE

by Jon Scieszka, Viking, 1991

Put a check on the line under AGREE if you agree with the statement. Put a check on the line under DISAGREE if you disagree with the statement.

AGREE   DISAGREE

______   ______   1. One can go back in time only in a story.

______   ______   2. Getting what you wish for is not always a good thing.

______   ______   3. Teasing an enemy isn't wise.

______   ______   4. Giants and dragons existed at one time in history.

______   ______   5. It is necessary to use your wits to avoid trouble.

______   ______   6. Refusing to fight is a wise thing to do.

______   ______   7. Accidents happen because people are careless.

______   ______   8. There were more cruel people in the Middle Ages than in our society today.

______   ______   9. Time-trekking back to the Middle Ages would be fun.

______   ______   10. Tricking people is a good way to get what you want.

______   ______   11. Sometimes it is hard to tell if you are dreaming or awake.

______   ______   12. Sometimes it's hard to explain your actions to a parent.

LIGHT IN THE FOREST

by Conrad Richter, Alfred A. Knopf, 1953

Put a check on the line under AGREE if you agree with the statement. Put a check on the line under DISAGREE if you disagree with the statement.

AGREE   DISAGREE

_____   _____   1. Your true parents are those who raised you, not those who gave you life.

_____   _____   2. Hatred is often expressed by silence.

_____   _____   3. Refusing an order is sometimes the best thing to do.

_____   _____   4. Sharing misery with a companion makes it easier to bear.

_____   _____   5. It is wiser to be willing and alive than defiant and dead.

_____   _____   6. The return of a captive raised from birth by American Indians is wrong.

_____   _____   7. American Indians thought that white people were uncivilized.

_____   _____   8. No person is ever truly free.

_____   _____   9. It takes a long time to unlearn what you have been taught for 10 years.

_____   _____   10. Injustice should be answered with violence.

_____   _____   11. You can make an Indian out of a white man but you can never make a white man out of an Indian.

_____   _____   12. Many people are slaves to the property they own

LILY'S CROSSING

by Patricia Reilly Giff, Delacorte, 1997

Put a check on the line under AGREE if you agree with the statement. Put a check on the line under DISAGREE if you disagree with the statement.

AGREE   DISAGREE

_______   _______   1. Even the firmest plans are changed when a nation goes to war.

_______   _______   2. A promise never to tell a lie is an impossible promise to keep.

_______   _______   3. Manners that seem strange to some people are quite acceptable to others.

_______   _______   4. Parents should not be allowed to join an armed service or go to war.

_______   _______   5. Deliberately avoiding someone means you have a guilty secret.

_______   _______   6. Most children don't realize how cruel it is to make fun of someone's attire.

_______   _______   7. Daydreaming can be a substitute for doing something you don't want to do.

_______   _______   8. A terrible day from start to finish means a better day ahead.

_______   _______   9. Sometimes a lie isn t really a lie.

_______   _______   10. There are many honest ways to acquire needed cash.

_______   _______   11. People argue over foolish issues simply because they like to argue.

_______   _______   12. War can make good companions of people who would not otherwise have been friends.

THE LION, THE WITCH AND THE WARDROBE

by C. S. Lewis, Macmillan, 1950

Put a check on the line under AGREE if you agree with the statement. Put a check on the line under DISAGREE if you disagree with the statement.

AGREE   DISAGREE

————   ————   1. Lands of eternal winter exist outside books.

————   ————   2. Old houses often reveal interesting secrets.

————   ————   3. The struggle between good and evil will never be fully resolved.

————   ————   4. Power can corrupt.

————   ————   5. Only people with closed minds refuse to believe the truth.

————   ————   6. Magical lands come alive only in books.

————   ————   7. The best place to hide something is in plain sight.

————   ————   8. Fairy tales are valuable because they stimulate the imagination.

————   ————   9. Without imagination there would be a total halt in all fields of human endeavor.

————   ————   10. The motive that would cause one person to betray another may be a good one.

————   ————   11. There were no children in London in World War II.

————   ————   12. A traitor should never be forgiven.

LITTLE HOUSE IN THE BIG WOODS

by Laura Ingalls Wilder, HarperCollins, 1953 (1932)

Put a check on the line under AGREE if you agree with the statement. Put a check on the line under DISAGREE if you disagree with the statement.

AGREE   DISAGREE

_______   _______   1. Living in a house surrounded by a big wood would be scary.

_______   _______   2. Winter was the most difficult time for pioneer families to get through.

_______   _______   3. In a pioneer family, different jobs were done on each day of the week.

_______   _______   4. Storytelling was the main source of entertainment in pioneer families.

_______   _______   5. Pioneers could not enjoy music because they had no radios or record player.

_______   _______   6. Late at night, it is easy to mistake a tree stump for a bear.

_______   _______   7. American tall tales were first told by the pioneers.

_______   _______   8. The most important possession of a pioneer family was a good gun.

_______   _______   9. If you hear a screech owl, bad luck will follow.

_______   _______   10. Pioneer children did not receive Christmas gifts because there were no stores where they could be purchased.

_______   _______   11. Pioneer children's birthdays were ignored.

_______   _______   12. Pioneer men often traded work with each other because no one man could be a Jack-of-all-trades.

LITTLE HOUSE ON THE PRAIRIE

by Laura Ingalls Wilder, HarperCollins, 1953 (1933)

Put a check on the line under AGREE if you agree with the statement. Put a check on the line under DISAGREE if you disagree with the statement.

AGREE   DISAGREE

_______   _______   1. Houses in the wilderness led to the disappearance of wildlife.

_______   _______   2. Crossing a fast-moving stream in a wagon is a good way to lose your life.

_______   _______   3. Losing a favorite pet is like losing a member of the family.

_______   _______   4. If you are a good listener, you may hear prairie music at night.

_______   _______   5. A house with no windows or doors would be a terrible place to live in.

_______   _______   6. Riding a horse in the middle of a wolf pack is a foolhardy thing to do.

_______   _______   7. When the fur on a dog's back stands up, good things are about to happen.

_______   _______   8. Living in a house with a dirt floor will make you sick.

_______   _______   9. Wading in a creek may be painful and dangerous.

_______   _______   10. There were some necessary foods that the pioneers could not produce.

_______   _______   11. Most pioneer families had access to a general store.

_______   _______   12. The American Indians and the pioneers fought each other because their beliefs were so different.

THE LITTLE PRINCE

by Antoine de Saint-Exupéry, Harcourt, Brace & World, 1943

Put a check on the line under AGREE if you agree with the statement. Put a check on the line under DISAGREE if you disagree with the statement.

AGREE   DISAGREE

_______   _______   1. Being alone and being lonely are not the same thing.

_______   _______   2. The important things in life are visible only to the heart.

_______   _______   3. Loving someone and accepting responsibility for that person go hand in hand.

_______   _______   4. Absence makes the heart grow fonder.

_______   _______   5. Catching someone in a lie means you will never again believe anything he or she says.

_______   _______   6. All human beings seek to be admired.

_______   _______   7. Most people do not see what is truly important in life.

_______   _______   8. An open-minded person leads a happier life than a closed-minded person does.

_______   _______   9. It is possible to be blind even though one has perfect vision.

_______   _______   10. Most people are not sensitive to the beauty of the world in which they live.

_______   _______   11. One can be an explorer without leaving home.

_______   _______   12. Every person has a responsibility to care for the planet he or she calls home.

LITTLE WOMEN

by Louisa May Alcott, Little, Brown, 1968 (1868)

Put a check on the line under AGREE if you agree with the statement. Put a check on the line under DISAGREE if you disagree with the statement.

AGREE   DISAGREE

_____   _____   1. Conflict between duty at home and personal growth will always exist for women.

_____   _____   2. Girls will be happier if they conform to the expectations of the society in which they live.

_____   _____   3. In the nineteenth century, the roles of men and women were more clearly defined than they are today.

_____   _____   4. Doing meaningful work is far more rewarding than seeking any kind of entertainment.

_____   _____   5. There is no happiness or satisfaction in getting revenge.

_____   _____   6. The best cure for unhappiness is hard work.

_____   _____   7. Poverty is a state of mind.

_____   _____   8. A person who helps others will always be rewarded.

_____   _____   9. Daily activities always seem boring after the holidays.

_____   _____   10. It is possible to insult another person without knowing it.

_____   _____   11. People are judged more often by their appearance than by what they say or do.

_____   _____   12. It is more difficult to write well using few words than using many words.

A LONG WAY FROM CHICAGO

by Richard Peck, Dial, 1997

Put a check on the line under AGREE if you agree with the statement. Put a check on the line under DISAGREE if you disagree with the statement.

AGREE   DISAGREE

_____   _____   1. Be cautious of rumors because they have wings.

_____   _____   2. There is no difference between an exaggeration and a lie.

_____   _____   3. Grandmothers are old women who spend their lives in rocking chairs.

_____   _____   4. Halloween pranks that cause work for others are not pranks but crimes that should be punished.

_____   _____   5. There is no difference between breaking a rule and breaking the law.

_____   _____   6. Prohibition, when alcohol was banned, was a very good thing.

_____   _____   7. When achieving a goal seems impossible, you should give up.

_____   _____   8. Matchmaking can be risky for all concerned.

_____   _____   9. Unconventional people don't care if they make others around them uncomfortable.

_____   _____   10. Growing up is often painful.

_____   _____   11. The only thing certain in life is change.

_____   _____   12. A grandmother who leads children into breaking the law should be jailed.

LORD OF THE DEEP

by Graham Salisbury, Delacorte, 2002

Put a check on the line under AGREE if you agree with the statement. Put a check on the line under DISAGREE if you disagree with the statement.

AGREE   DISAGREE

_____   _____   1. An older brother should always let a handicapped younger brother have his way.

_____   _____   2. Killing wild creatures is wrong unless they are the only available source of food.

_____   _____   3. To be idolized is a very uncomfortable feeling.

_____   _____   4. Anyone put on a pedestal is destined for a fall.

_____   _____   5. It is okay to tell a lie as long as no one is hurt by it.

_____   _____   6. When money is in short supply, people will compromise their principles to get it.

_____   _____   7. Being the best at what you do is both a blessing and a curse.

_____   _____   8. One who runs a business is obliged to put up with obnoxious customers.

_____   _____   9. Learning new skills can be frustrating and rewarding at the same time.

_____   _____   10. When someone you admire disappoints you, forgive and forget.

_____   _____   11. To be a successful deep-sea fisherman, one must have both know-how and strength.

_____   _____   12. Standing up for what is right may cause you to lose the things you value.

LYDDIE

by Katherine Paterson, Dutton, Lodestar Books, 1991

Put a check on the line under AGREE if you agree with the statement. Put a check on the line under DISAGREE if you disagree with the statement.

AGREE   DISAGREE

_____   _____   1. Without religious freedom, there can be no other freedoms.

_____   _____   2. Leaving a familiar home for a new one is both painful and exciting.

_____   _____   3. Only uneducated people are superstitious.

_____   _____   4. Without a library, a town would be narrow minded.

_____   _____   5. A factory owner who ignores poor working conditions is cutting into his own profit.

_____   _____   6. A petition is a valuable method of bringing about positive change.

_____   _____   7. It is foolish to work hard to pay off someone else's debt.

_____   _____   8. In 1843, a factory girl's life was very like that of a slave.

_____   _____   9. Some people do not have the ability to learn new mechanical skills.

_____   _____   10. A true friend would not ask you to do something risky.

_____   _____   11. People who support radical causes are born troublemakers.

_____   _____   12. Standing up for what is right may cause you to lose the things you value.

M. C. HIGGINS THE GREAT

by *Virginia Hamilton,* Macmillan, 1975

Put a check on the line under AGREE if you agree with the statement. Put a check on the line under DISAGREE if you disagree with the statement.

AGREE   DISAGREE

_____   _____   1. Strip mining should be banned because it destroys the environment.

_____   _____   2. If you dream long enough about something, your dream will come true.

_____   _____   3. No one else can change your life. Only you can do that.

_____   _____   4. Every person needs time alone to dream.

_____   _____   5. You should avoid strangers, even if you need help.

_____   _____   6. A mountain may be a character in a novel.

_____   _____   7. Every human being keeps hidden the characteristics that he or she does not want others to see.

_____   _____   8. No one truly owns land. He or she is merely a caretaker of it.

_____   _____   9. A good place to survey the world is from the top of a 40-foot steel pole.

_____   _____   10. Everyone would like to have a mother who is a singing star.

_____   _____   11. Hiking is one of the most satisfying outdoor sports.

_____   _____   12. Some people live in the past and in the future at the same time.

THE MAGICIAN'S NEPHEW

by C. S. Lewis, Harper & Row, 1955

Put a check on the line under AGREE if you agree with the statement. Put a check on the line under DISAGREE if you disagree with the statement.

AGREE   DISAGREE

_______   _______   1. A secretive person has evil deeds to hide.

_______   _______   2. Facing your fears can overcome all that life throws at you.

_______   _______   3. Playing a trick on someone is acceptable if you know the outcome will be pleasant.

_______   _______   4. A manipulative person has no care for the feelings of others.

_______   _______   5. One who does not keep up with the times will often make unreasonable requests.

_______   _______   6. Never undertake an action without knowing its likely result.

_______   _______   7. The best way to deal with a person who is out of control is to speak softly and give in to his or her demands.

_______   _______   8. Taking action against someone will often hurt people who are not the intended victim.

_______   _______   9. The Earth belongs to everyone, and everyone has a responsibility to keep it clean and growing.

_______   _______   10. No matter how long it takes, good will always triumph over evil.

_______   _______   11. A person who forgives will reap greater rewards than the person who is forgiven.

_______   _______   12. Life's problems cannot be solved by magic but only by common sense and hard work.

MANIAC MAGEE

by Jerry Spinelli, Little, Brown, 1990

Put a check on the line under AGREE if you agree with the statement. Put a check on the line under DISAGREE if you disagree with the statement.

AGREE   DISAGREE

_____   _____   1. Some relatives who live together don't like each other.

_____   _____   2. When you are hungry and have no money, a garbage can may be a good place to find food.

_____   _____   3. Most towns have sections it is best to stay out of.

_____   _____   4. A torn book page is like a bird's broken wing.

_____   _____   5. You should avoid strangers, even if you need help.

_____   _____   6. If you are surrounded by toughs who want something you have, give it to them.

_____   _____   7. It is not possible to live comfortably in two totally different cultures.

_____   _____   8. People who love noise and colors are scatterbrained.

_____   _____   9. Never admit that you don't have a home.

_____   _____   10. Staying with your own kind means you will never grow and change.

_____   _____   11. It is not always possible to tell if someone dislikes you.

_____   _____   12. Accepting a dare is always foolish.

MATILDA

by Roald Dahl, Puffin Books, 1988

Put a check on the line under AGREE if you agree with the statement. Put a check on the line under DISAGREE if you disagree with the statement.

AGREE   DISAGREE

______   ______   1. Some four-year-olds read quite well.

______   ______   2. Some teachers really do not like children.

______   ______   3. Physical punishment should be done away with in all schools.

______   ______   4. Some parents are more concerned with their own pleasures than with their children's welfare.

______   ______   5. Reading is far more exciting than watching television.

______   ______   6. Selling an old car by telling the customer it is in perfect condition when it is not is the same as stealing.

______   ______   7. Some problems need drastic measures in order to be solved.

______   ______   8. Some people are able to solve difficult math problems in their heads.

______   ______   9. Sometimes being very small has its advantages.

______   ______   10. Some people can make things move by looking at them.

______   ______   11. First-grade teachers are more approachable than upper-grade teachers.

______   ______   12. A genius is a person with unusual mental abilities.

MAX AND ME AND THE TIME MACHINE

by Gery Greer, Harcourt Brace Jovanovich, 1983

Put a check on the line under AGREE if you agree with the statement. Put a check on the line under DISAGREE if you disagree with the statement.

AGREE   DISAGREE

_____   _____   1. Time machines exist only in fantasy literature.

_____   _____   2. It is possible to have a reputation without having the skills associated with it.

_____   _____   3. When an opponent seems too tough, the best thing to do is run away.

_____   _____   4. Be kind to people of lower rank, for one day they may outrank you.

_____   _____   5. Being transported to another time in history would be exciting.

_____   _____   6. Never enter a contest you are not prepared to win.

_____   _____   7. When things don't go exactly as planned, change your plans.

_____   _____   8. Never allow someone to put words into your mouth.

_____   _____   9. Laughter is cruel when you are the object of the joke.

_____   _____   10. When you don't want to give direct answers, pretend you don't understand the questions.

_____   _____   11. An untrue accusation may lead to violence.

_____   _____   12. A secret room isn't secret if more than one person knows about it.

MEDICINE WALK

by Ardath Mayhar, Atheneum, 1985

Put a check on the line under AGREE if you agree with the statement. Put a check on the line under DISAGREE if you disagree with the statement.

AGREE   DISAGREE

_____   _____   1. Deliberately flying off course in a small plane is a way to court disaster.

_____   _____   2. Leaving the safety of a plane for an unknown wilderness would be foolish.

_____   _____   3. No one can survive walking 40 miles in the desert.

_____   _____   4. Running five miles before school means you will sleep during lessons.

_____   _____   5. The Earth's gifts are not given freely.

_____   _____   6. The greatest need of a human being in the desert is food.

_____   _____   7. Some experiences can change one overnight.

_____   _____   8. When you know you can't succeed, it is time to give up.

_____   _____   9. The sounds of wild night creatures can be comforting when you are all alone.

_____   _____   10. At night, a burning desert turns into an icebox.

_____   _____   11. Sometimes it is necessary to separate the mind from the body.

_____   _____   12. A feeling of sheer terror takes away all reasoning powers.

MIRACLES ON MAPLE HILL

by Karen Ackerman, Harcourt, Brace, 1956

Put a check on the line under AGREE if you agree with the statement. Put a check on the line under DISAGREE if you disagree with the statement.

AGREE   DISAGREE

_____   _____   1. War changes those who have to fight.

_____   _____   2. There is no such thing as a miracle.

_____   _____   3. Bickering among brothers and sisters is natural.

_____   _____   4. Old houses often contain hidden treasures.

_____   _____   5. Most people do not follow the rules of healthy living.

_____   _____   6. Farm children work harder and work longer hours than city children.

_____   _____   7. Most people live alone because they choose to.

_____   _____   8. Having warm weather all year round would be great.

_____   _____   9. It is very difficult to change someone s thinking.

_____   _____   10. Fire is a danger in old farmhouses.

_____   _____   11. A hero is someone who is never afraid.

_____   _____   12. Country neighbors help each other more than city neighbors do.

THE MISADVENTURES OF MAUDE MARCH

by Audrey Couloumbis, Random House, 2005

Put a check on the line under AGREE if you agree with the statement. Put a check on the line under DISAGREE if you disagree with the statement.

AGREE   DISAGREE

______   ______   1. Sometimes being polite can get you into trouble.

______   ______   2. It was not unusual to hear gunshots in the Old West.

______   ______   3. Old people are boring when they recall events from the past.

______   ______   4. Leaving familiar surroundings may be either frightening or challenging but not both.

______   ______   5. You should never make a choice for other people, even when they are unwilling to choose for themselves.

______   ______   6. Never try to act like another person; always be yourself.

______   ______   7. Sometimes criminals give the best advice.

______   ______   8. Only a person with something to hide would wear a disguise.

______   ______   9. It is okay to take something that isn't yours if you are recovering it for the owner.

______   ______   10. Never stand by and do nothing if you see someone being treated badly.

______   ______   11. It is possible to make it through the night in a snowstorm without a fire.

______   ______   12. People are capable of doing much more than they think they can do.

THE MISERABLE MILL

by Lemony Snicket, HarperCollins, 2001

Put a check on the line under AGREE if you agree with the statement. Put a check on the line under DISAGREE if you disagree with the statement.

AGREE   DISAGREE

_____   _____   1. Some towns are so dark and dreary that no resident ever smiles.

_____   _____   2. Orphans have no control over the place where they will live.

_____   _____   3. Finding your way about in a strange place can be an adventure.

_____   _____   4. A door that has not been opened for 14 years must hide a terrible secret.

_____   _____   5. Families can face any hardship if they stick together.

_____   _____   6. Backbreaking labor can lead to strong bones and teeth.

_____   _____   7. It is not possible to change your personality.

_____   _____   8. Factory accidents happen because of carelessness.

_____   _____   9. No one would deliberately try to cause an injury to another.

_____   _____   10. A bully is a person with low self-esteem.

_____   _____   11. When an adult won't listen, yell louder.

_____   _____   12. No one wants to read a story with an unhappy ending.

MISS HICKORY

by Carolyn Sherwin Bailey, Viking, 1946

Put a check on the line under AGREE if you agree with the statement. Put a check on the line under DISAGREE if you disagree with the statement.

AGREE   DISAGREE

_______   _______   1. An unwelcome visitor can upset a household's routine.

_______   _______   2. Thick fur on a caterpillar is a sign of a severe winter.

_______   _______   3. Moving to a new home is fun when a friend is willing to help.

_______   _______   4. The greatest enemy of a hickory-nut doll is a squirrel.

_______   _______   5. There is always safety in numbers.

_______   _______   6. Birds cannot survive winter without the help of people.

_______   _______   7. A fawn that loses its mother will not survive.

_______   _______   8. When a groundhog sees its shadow, there will be six more weeks of winter.

_______   _______   9. Children who tease wild animals are asking for trouble.

_______   _______   10. New clothes make one feel like a new person.

_______   _______   11. A robin's nest is a good winter home for a hickory doll.

_______   _______   12. If an enemy invites you to a party, don't go.

THE MISSING GATOR OF GUMBO LIMBO

by Jean Craighead George, HarperCollins, 1992

Put a check on the line under AGREE if you agree with the statement. Put a check on the line under DISAGREE if you disagree with the statement.

AGREE   DISAGREE

1. Some people prefer to live in the woods instead of in a house.

2. A child punished for no reason will try to get even.

3. Some animals are protected by law because people don't care if they become extinct.

4. People escape from society because they are lazy and don't want to work.

5. Poets view the world differently from other people.

6. Seeing the world from the top of a tree gives one a greater appreciation of nature.

7. It is okay to trick someone when you have good intentions.

8. When many people move into a wildlife area, the wildlife disappears.

9. Protecting the environment is a job best left to conservationists.

10. It is impossible to get a government official to solve a problem.

11. One reason for not giving a correct address is that you don't have an address.

12. It is everyone's responsibility to protect the environment.

MISSING MAY

by Cynthia Rylant, Orchard Books, Richard Jackson, 1993

Put a check on the line under AGREE if you agree with the statement. Put a check on the line under DISAGREE if you disagree with the statement.

AGREE   DISAGREE

______   ______   1. Spending quality time with someone means having that person's full attention.

______   ______   2. A truly kind person would never raise his or her voice.

______   ______   3. Never love anyone, because some day you might lose that person.

______   ______   4. It is never possible to fill another person s shoes.

______   ______   5. Revealing secrets is acceptable if no harm is intended.

______   ______   6. Revealing secrets is never acceptable.

______   ______   7. Being alone and being lonely are not the same thing.

______   ______   8. High expectations may become shattered dreams.

______   ______   9. No question is a stupid question.

______   ______   10. Grief and self-pity are the same thing.

______   ______   11. A garden is more than just growing plants.

______   ______   12. The greatest gift one can give a child is love.

MOLLY'S PILGRIM

by Barbara Cohen, Lothrop, Lee & Shepard, 1983

Put a check on the line under AGREE if you agree with the statement. Put a check on the line under DISAGREE if you disagree with the statement.

AGREE   DISAGREE

_____   _____   1. Being a new student in a school is an unhappy experience.

_____   _____   2. A child who dresses differently is often an object of ridicule.

_____   _____   3. It is possible to be an honor student in one school and a failing student in another.

_____   _____   4. Children who tease others because of their speech or appearance don't really mean to be cruel.

_____   _____   5. A Pilgrim is any person who comes to a new land, whether long ago or today.

_____   _____   6. Parents understand more than their children think they do.

_____   _____   7. Often a child is torn between obeying a parent's wishes and wanting to be part of a group.

_____   _____   8. Keeping up family traditions is an important part of life.

_____   _____   9. A kind teacher can make the transition to a new school easier.

_____   _____   10. Learning a new language is easier for children than for adults.

_____   _____   11. It takes all kinds of Pilgrims to make a Thanksgiving.

_____   _____   12. Listen to your parents; they are always right.

MONKEY ISLAND

by Paula Fox, Orchard Books, 1991

Put a check on the line under AGREE if you agree with the statement. Put a check on the line under DISAGREE if you disagree with the statement.

AGREE   DISAGREE

_____   _____   1. Homeless people are homeless because they choose to be.

_____   _____   2. People on welfare would rather be earning a living.

_____   _____   3. Shelters for the homeless are dangerous places.

_____   _____   4. No one likes to be hugged by someone he or she doesn't know.

_____   _____   5. Only a loving parent would give up a child if the child would receive better care from another person.

_____   _____   6. Every large city has tried to get rid of street people without success.

_____   _____   7. A city park at night can be a very dangerous place.

_____   _____   8. An ageless person is one who is tolerant of many lifestyles.

_____   _____   9. It is impossible to care about someone you don't like.

_____   _____   10. Sleep does not always banish tiredness.

_____   _____   11. People who have little are more likely to share than those who have a lot.

_____   _____   12. The job of a social-service worker is to care for people who cannot care for themselves.

THE MOORCHILD

by Eloise McGraw, Simon & Schuster, 1997

Put a check on the line under AGREE if you agree with the statement. Put a check on the line under DISAGREE if you disagree with the statement.

AGREE   DISAGREE

_______   _______   1. First impressions based on the appearance of others are usually right.

_______   _______   2. It is possible for some people to play a musical instrument well without any instruction.

_______   _______   3. A changeling would appear only in a fantasy tale.

_______   _______   4. Parents would always know if someone switched their baby with another.

_______   _______   5. Sometimes there is nothing you can do to fit into the community where you live.

_______   _______   6. A group will often perform unkind acts that an individual in the group would not perform on his or her own.

_______   _______   7. Friendship may grow out of initial dislike and distrust.

_______   _______   8. A person may become the object of intense hatred without doing anything to cause such feelings.

_______   _______   9. All human beings need someone with whom they can relax and be themselves.

_______   _______   10. Being alone and being lonely are not the same thing.

_______   _______   11. Escaping to a place in the natural world will help sort out your troubles.

_______   _______   12. A changeling is an evil person who should be shunned by society.

THE MOUSE AND THE MOTORCYCLE

by Beverly Cleary, William Morrow, 1965

Put a check on the line under AGREE if you agree with the statement. Put a check on the line under DISAGREE if you disagree with the statement.

AGREE   DISAGREE

______   ______   1. A long car trip can be an exciting adventure.

______   ______   2. Having a hotel room all to yourself is scary.

______   ______   3. Dogs and mice are natural enemies.

______   ______   4. Some people have a habit of losing things because they want attention.

______   ______   5. When an owl sees a mouse, it tries to make friends.

______   ______   6. Sharing what you have with others is not always a good idea.

______   ______   7. When relatives come to visit, it is time to hide.

______   ______   8. It is foolish to put yourself in danger to help another person.

______   ______   9. A person who makes an honest mistake should be quickly forgiven, even if the mistake harms someone.

______   ______   10. A hero must always be very brave and unafraid.

______   ______   11. The more difficult a task is, the more pride one takes in accomplishing it.

______   ______   12. A mouse is safer inside a house than out in the woods.

MR. CHICKEN'S FUNNY MONEY

by Christopher Paul Curtis, Wendy Lamb Books, 2005

Put a check on the line under AGREE if you agree with the statement. Put a check on the line under DISAGREE if you disagree with the statement.

AGREE   DISAGREE

_____   _____   1. A bill with 15 zeros on it could not possibly be correct.

_____   _____   2. A man who talks into his watch must be mentally disturbed.

_____   _____   3. One could not be a jet fighter pilot during the Civil War.

_____   _____   4. Parents who answer a question with a question don't know the answer.

_____   _____   5. It is always wise to steer clear of a wet dog.

_____   _____   6. In a civilized society, adults have all the power.

_____   _____   7. Money can change personalities and make people act as they would not otherwise act.

_____   _____   8. The only people you can really trust are your parents, because they alone are concerned for your welfare.

_____   _____   9. The most important act in making a decision is to weigh the evidence.

_____   _____   10. If parents say something you don't want to hear, pretend you don't understand.

_____   _____   11. Part of being a great detective is being flexible in your thinking.

_____   _____   12. If you swallow food whole, you will never get cavities.

MR. LINCOLN'S DRUMMER BOY

by G. Clifton Wisler, Scholastic, 1995

Put a check on the line under AGREE if you agree with the statement. Put a check on the line under DISAGREE if you disagree with the statement.

AGREE   DISAGREE

_____   _____   1. Eleven-year-olds could join the Union Army in 1861.

_____   _____   2. More Union soldiers died from disease than from bullets.

_____   _____   3. War is an exciting adventure.

_____   _____   4. Whether chores at home are fun or not depends on your attitude.

_____   _____   5. Young children should never be allowed to play war games.

_____   _____   6. It is impossible to live outdoors in winter.

_____   _____   7. It would be impossible to live in a city without electricity.

_____   _____   8. Exploring a strange place would be an exciting adventure.

_____   _____   9. Running away from home with no place to go is foolish.

_____   _____   10. A person who is afraid cannot be courageous.

_____   _____   11. There can never be a good reason for war.

_____   _____   12. Returning home after a year away, you would expect to find everything just as you left it.

MR. POPPER'S PENGUINS

by Florence and Richard Atwater, Little, Brown, 1938

Put a check on the line under AGREE if you agree with the statement. Put a check on the line under DISAGREE if you disagree with the statement.

AGREE   DISAGREE

_______   _______ 1. It is possible to be a world traveler in an armchair.

_______   _______ 2. Without television there is nothing to do on a winter evening.

_______   _______ 3. One should never have a wild animal as a pet.

_______   _______ 4. Anything that disrupts an entire house should be removed.

_______   _______ 5. Responsible pet owners do not have more than one pet.

_______   _______ 6. Pets can be a problem even when they receive good care.

_______   _______ 7. Getting information from city hall can be difficult.

_______   _______ 8. When things disappear from a house, you know a thief has been at work.

_______   _______ 9. Fame means happiness.

_______   _______ 10. Being in the wrong place at the wrong time is not always a bad thing.

_______   _______ 11. Just when things seem at their worst, something good is bound to happen.

_______   _______ 12. Living happily ever after happens only in a fantasy tale.

MR. REVERE AND I

by Robert Lawson, Little, Brown, 1953

Put a check on the line under AGREE if you agree with the statement. Put a check on the line under DISAGREE if you disagree with the statement.

AGREE   DISAGREE

_____   _____   1. No one would like to be on a ship at sea for more than a month.

_____   _____   2. A person who abuses an animal can't help it, because such a person was not taught kindness as a child.

_____   _____   3. When you know you are not welcome, the best thing to do is leave.

_____   _____   4. It is always difficult to adapt to a new neighborhood.

_____   _____   5. Watching a military parade reminds people that a nation without an army would not need to go to war.

_____   _____   6. When a horse "approaches the home stretch," this means it will win the race.

_____   _____   7. Gambling can lead to many losses other than money.

_____   _____   8. People should be proud to pay taxes, because the money is used for the good of the country.

_____   _____   9. Anything can be learned with determination and constant practice.

_____   _____   10. If you are in "the calm before a storm," good things are going to happen.

_____   _____   11. Independence makes a person responsible for his or her actions.

_____   _____   12. Victory against all odds is very unusual.

MRS. FRISBY AND THE RATS OF NIMH

by Robert O'Brien, HarperCollins, 1986

Put a check on the line under AGREE if you agree with the statement. Put a check on the line under DISAGREE if you disagree with the statement.

AGREE   DISAGREE

_______   _______   1. Many mothers are forced to raise their children alone.

_______   _______   2. Sometimes an impossible situation has no solution.

_______   _______   3. Scientists should never use animals in their experiments.

_______   _______   4. Rats can be taught to read.

_______   _______   5. There are civilizations in existence that we know nothing about.

_______   _______   6. Sometimes it is necessary to speak to someone you fear.

_______   _______   7. Learning to read is like walking through a giant maze.

_______   _______   8. A mother would break the law to protect her child.

_______   _______   9. Farmers do not care about disturbing wildlife when they plow their fields.

_______   _______   10. Rodents can destroy a farmer s crop and should be eliminated.

_______   _______   11. It is foolish to help someone you don't know.

_______   _______   12. Many animals are highly intelligent.

MUGGIE MAGGIE

by Beverly Cleary, Morrow Junior Books, 1990

Put a check on the line under AGREE if you agree with the statement. Put a check on the line under DISAGREE if you disagree with the statement.

AGREE   DISAGREE

_____   _____   1. One who teases younger children has little self-esteem.

_____   _____   2. Cursive writing is more difficult to do than printing.

_____   _____   3. A person who is contrary never changes.

_____   _____   4. When the teacher asks a parent for a conference, trouble follows.

_____   _____   5. A dog in the school playground is a welcome visitor.

_____   _____   6. A gifted, talented person is hard to get along with.

_____   _____   7. When stubbornness goes too far, friends are lost.

_____   _____   8. When someone pushes a table at you, push back!

_____   _____   9. When a nickname sticks, it can hurt the person to whom it is given.

_____   _____   10. You always know when a parent means what he or she says.

_____   _____   11. The best gift to receive is the gift of friendship.

_____   _____   12. When you know you are right, don't give in, regardless of pressure from parents or friends.

THE MUSIC OF DOLPHINS

by Karen Hesse, Scholastic, 1998

Put a check on the line under AGREE if you agree with the statement. Put a check on the line under DISAGREE if you disagree with the statement.

AGREE   DISAGREE

_______   _______   1. Newspapers thrive on unusual occurrences.

_______   _______   2. A girl stranded on an unpopulated island for nine years would welcome rescue.

_______   _______   3. It is possible for a human being to be raised by dolphins.

_______   _______   4. Learning to speak a new language is more difficult for older children than for younger children.

_______   _______   5. Learning new rules and meeting new expectations are very frustrating and difficult.

_______   _______   6. Dolphins are highly intelligent creatures.

_______   _______   7. Human beings must expect many disappointments in life.

_______   _______   8. Scientists have a right to study human beings without permission if it furthers scientific knowledge.

_______   _______   9. You cannot force anyone to learn something he or she does not want to learn.

_______   _______   10. It is possible to belong to two worlds and to show love and loyalty to both.

_______   _______   11. There are many similarities between human life and dolphin life.

_______   _______   12. No one can resist trying to find out what is behind a locked door.

MY BROTHER SAM IS DEAD

by James Lincoln Collier and
Christopher Collier, Four Winds, 1974

Put a check on the line under AGREE if you agree with the statement. Put a check on the line under DISAGREE if you disagree with the statement.

AGREE   DISAGREE

______   ______   1. If nations had no weapons, there would be no wars.

______   ______   2. The British lost the Revolutionary War because they did not know how to fight.

______   ______   3. It is unfair to tax people who cannot vote on how the taxes are to be spent.

______   ______   4. Many of the early colonists were loyal to England.

______   ______   5. War is a romantic adventure for the young men who sign up to fight.

______   ______   6. Members of the same family may be on different sides of a war.

______   ______   7. Stealing a gun is wrong, even if it is for a good cause.

______   ______   8. Some family disagreements can never be settled.

______   ______   9. Only a highly disturbed boy would point a gun at his brother.

______   ______   10. Political issues may divide a close family.

______   ______   11. Becoming an adult is not a matter of age, but a matter of accepting responsibility for your actions.

______   ______   12. People are often accused of crimes they did not commit.

MY DANIEL

by Pam Conrad, HarperCollins, 1989

Put a check on the line under AGREE if you agree with the statement. Put a check on the line under DISAGREE if you disagree with the statement.

AGREE   DISAGREE

_______   _______   1. Museums are boring places to visit.

_______   _______   2. No one looks forward to having relatives come to visit.

_______   _______   3. Treasures can be found in the dirt if you dig deep enough.

_______   _______   4. Elderly people do not like to travel far from home.

_______   _______   5. No one wants to hear the stories that grandparents tell about when they were young.

_______   _______   6. Everyone should have a dream to hold on to.

_______   _______   7. Being home alone in a storm can be a thrilling experience.

_______   _______   8. Nearly every family has something very old that it treasures.

_______   _______   9. Some things are so precious that they must be kept hidden.

_______   _______   10. Rules are made to be broken.

_______   _______   11. There are times when it is impossible to avoid trouble in a public place.

_______   _______   12. Every family should cherish its family history.

MY SIDE OF THE MOUNTAIN

by Jean Craighead George, HarperCollins, 1972

Put a check on the line under AGREE if you agree with the statement. Put a check on the line under DISAGREE if you disagree with the statement.

AGREE   DISAGREE

———   ———   1. Living alone in the mountains would be exciting.

———   ———   2. A city boy spending a night in the woods would want to return to the city.

———   ———   3. A good way to discover if wild plants are edible is to taste them.

———   ———   4. A human voice may sound strange in the wilderness.

———   ———   5. Taming a wild bird is impossible.

———   ———   6. Trapping animals is cruel and inhuman.

———   ———   7. A hollow tree in the woods is a good place to live.

———   ———   8. To be like Thoreau is to love nature.

———   ———   9. Holidays are never celebrated in the wild.

———   ———   10. The woods after an ice storm are less dangerous than a city after an ice storm.

———   ———   11. The best gift for a woodsman would be a hatchet.

———   ———   12. There are disadvantages to being totally independent.

NETTIE'S TRIP SOUTH

by Ann Turner, Macmillan, 1987

Put a check on the line under AGREE if you agree with the statement. Put a check on the line under DISAGREE if you disagree with the statement.

AGREE   DISAGREE

———   ———   1. Everyone should have one good friend to talk to.

———   ———   2. Traveling to a new place can be scary and exciting at the same time.

———   ———   3. Before the Civil War, many slaves had only one name.

———   ———   4. Slaves smiled at their masters to hide their resentment.

———   ———   5. Slave children were sold away from their parents.

———   ———   6. There is never a valid reason why one human being should own another.

———   ———   7. You can embarrass another person without intending to.

———   ———   8. Older brothers get irritated at their little sisters' questions.

———   ———   9. Slaves were forbidden to learn to read for fear they would become smarter than their masters.

———   ———   10. Some times it is good to give wrong answers to questions.

———   ———   11. There are many sights children should not be allowed to see.

———   ———   12. Bad dreams may be caused by the cruel actions of others.

NIGHT CROSSING

by Karen Ackerman, Alfred A. Knopf, 1994

Put a check on the line under AGREE if you agree with the statement. Put a check on the line under DISAGREE if you disagree with the statement.

AGREE   DISAGREE

1. People suffer when an enemy occupies a country.

2. Applying rules to just one group of people is acceptable in wartime.

3. Laws that prevent people from practicing their religion should be abolished.

4. Going to live in a new land can be frightening.

5. Sometimes it is necessary to hide from others.

6. A cheap bracelet may become valuable.

7. Family safety is more important than possessions.

8. In World War II, the Nazis persecuted the Jewish people.

9. It would be great not to be allowed to go to school.

10. Sometimes it is good to give wrong answers to questions.

11. Some people will risk their lives to save the life of a friend.

12. Eavesdropping is not always wrong.

THE NIGHT JOURNEY

by Kathryn Lasky, Viking, 1986

Put a check on the line under AGREE if you agree with the statement. Put a check on the line under DISAGREE if you disagree with the statement.

AGREE   DISAGREE

______   ______   1. Teens don't want to listen to the stories their grandparents or great-grandparents tell abut their lives.

______   ______   2. Events that took place before you were born have no effect on your life today.

______   ______   3. Having to babysit an aging relative is a boring job.

______   ______   4. It is usually best not to remember sad events in the past.

______   ______   5. Cooperation is essential to success.

______   ______   6. A person with eyes that frighten others has seen terrible things in his or her past.

______   ______   7. It is possible to be brave in one situation and cowardly in another.

______   ______   8. It is important to pass family stories on to younger generations.

______   ______   9. There are times when escape from danger requires the clever thinking of a child.

______   ______   10. At the turn of the twentieth century, entire villages in Russia were destroyed by the czar's armies.

______   ______   11. A teapot can be a symbol of friendship and comfort.

______   ______   12. People who must flee for their lives often take meaningful but useless objects with them.

NIGHTJOHN

by Gary Paulsen, Delacorte, 1993

Put a check on the line under AGREE if you agree with the statement. Put a check on the line under DISAGREE if you disagree with the statement.

AGREE   DISAGREE

______   ______   1. Plantation owners thought slaves who could read were dangerous.

______   ______   2. Today, as in the past, reading is the first step toward freedom.

______   ______   3. It would be foolish to risk your life simply to teach someone to read.

______   ______   4. Some escaped slaves deliberately returned to slavery.

______   ______   5. Listening to others' conversations when they don't know you are there is not always wrong.

______   ______   6. Freedom and prosperity go hand in hand.

______   ______   7. A little knowledge can be a dangerous thing.

______   ______   8. Most slaves did not try to run away.

______   ______   9. Reading and writing can lead to rebellion.

______   ______   10. Throughout history, some people have risked their lives for an education.

______   ______   11. Many slaves had first names but no last names.

______   ______   12. A slave's working day could be 16 hours or more.

NIGHT OF THE TWISTERS

by Ivy Ruckman, Crowell, 1984

Put a check on the line under AGREE if you agree with the statement. Put a check on the line under DISAGREE if you disagree with the statement.

AGREE   DISAGREE

_______   _______   1. Money would be the best thing to win in a contest.

_______   _______   2. You don't really appreciate what you have until you lose it.

_______   _______   3. Tornado warnings can be ignored, since twisters rarely touch the ground.

_______   _______   4. A new baby in the house changes everyone's life.

_______   _______   5. Think twice before accepting a friend's invitation to stay overnight.

_______   _______   6. A tornado can wipe out an entire town.

_______   _______   7. Many older children resent their younger brothers and sisters.

_______   _______   8. When a tornado strikes, the best place to be is under a tree away from the house.

_______   _______   9. Living in the past is better than looking toward an uncertain future.

_______   _______   10. People left homeless by a tornado should not rebuild, since another tornado could level their new home.

_______   _______   11. It is the duty of every citizen to help clean up after a natural disaster.

_______   _______   12. After a tornado hits, the disaster area is a very dangerous place to be.

NORY RYAN'S SONG

by Patricia Reilly Giff, Random House, 2002

Put a check on the line under AGREE if you agree with the statement. Put a check on the line under DISAGREE if you disagree with the statement.

AGREE   DISAGREE

_______   _______   1. Between 1845 and 1852, over a million Irish people died of starvation.

_______   _______   2. Leaving a familiar home for a new one is both painful and exciting and requires a good deal of courage.

_______   _______   3. A terrible smell in the middle of the night always means disaster.

_______   _______   4. Nothing is ever given without cost, even though it seems to be free.

_______   _______   5. It is impossible to have hope when death and cruelty are all around you.

_______   _______   6. When starvation looms in a community, neighbors turn on each other.

_______   _______   7. It is not uncommon for a family member to risk his or her life to save other members of the family.

_______   _______   8. In today's world of plenty there are no starving nations.

_______   _______   9. The person who is the heart of the family is not always one of the parents.

_______   _______   10. A starving person will eat seaweed and grass for nourishment.

_______   _______   11. During the potato-famine years, the British sent food across the sea and let the Irish starve.

_______   _______   12. Only a charlatan uses herbs to cure sickness.

NOTHING BUT THE TRUTH

by Avi, Orchard Books, 1991

Put a check on the line under AGREE if you agree with the statement. Put a check on the line under DISAGREE if you disagree with the statement.

AGREE   DISAGREE

_____   _____   1. Public address systems in schools are annoying and should be eliminated.

_____   _____   2. A person who becomes a class clown is insecure.

_____   _____   3. It is possible to have high grades in math and low grades in English.

_____   _____   4. Only a kid who is out of control refuses to follow school rules.

_____   _____   5. A teacher who knows his or her subject well deserves respect.

_____   _____   6. Defying authority may lead to a change in the rules.

_____   _____   7. High test scores by students indicate a good teacher.

_____   _____   8. Students suspended from school will get into trouble on the streets.

_____   _____   9. Slanting a news story means not reporting the facts.

_____   _____   10. Public opinion can be a powerful force for good or evil.

_____   _____   11. People who phone in to talk shows do so to get attention.

_____   _____   12. Some people choose not to exercise a hard-won freedom.

NUMBER THE STARS

by Lois Lowry, Houghton Mifflin, 1980

Put a check on the line under AGREE if you agree with the statement. Put a check on the line under DISAGREE if you disagree with the statement.

AGREE   DISAGREE

_______   _______   1. An occupied town should not engage in open resistance to the enemy.

_______   _______   2. A country with no army has no choice but to surrender when an enemy attacks.

_______   _______   3. During World War II, many people were persecuted because of their religion.

_______   _______   4. The greatest enemy of a people is fear.

_______   _______   5. Rationing is a necessary part of wartime.

_______   _______   6. Surrendering is often better than fighting.

_______   _______   7. Pounding on a door late at night usually means good news.

_______   _______   8. Deception is acceptable when lives are at stake.

_______   _______   9. A good definition of bravery is facing the enemy even though you are afraid.

_______   _______   10. Most people are willing to confront danger when freedom is threatened.

_______   _______   11. Books of facts are more important than stories.

_______   _______   12. It is always wrong to pretend to be someone you are not.

OLD YELLER

by Fred Gipson, Harper & Row, 1956

Put a check on the line under AGREE if you agree with the statement. Put a check on the line under DISAGREE if you disagree with the statement.

AGREE   DISAGREE

______   ______   1. A fourteen-year-old boy can handle a man's responsibilities.

______   ______   2. Little brothers can be a pain.

______   ______   3. It is okay to kill an animal for food.

______   ______   4. A dog that steals food should be shot.

______   ______   5. A dog bitten by a rabid animal must be killed.

______   ______   6. Rounding up and marking wild hogs is a dangerous job.

______   ______   7. Not facing up to facts means trouble.

______   ______   8. Drastic measures must sometimes be taken to keep a disease from spreading.

______   ______   9. Catching a bear cub is not a good idea.

______   ______   10. Ignoring a warning is asking for trouble.

______   ______   11. A woman can do any job a man can do.

______   ______   12. It is possible to be numb with grief.

OLIVE'S OCEAN

by Kevin Henkes, Greenwillow Books, 2003

Put a check on the line under AGREE if you agree with the statement. Put a check on the line under DISAGREE if you disagree with the statement.

AGREE   DISAGREE

_____   _____   1. Every class has a quiet student that no one knows or thinks about.

_____   _____   2. Never answer the door if a stranger rings the bell.

_____   _____   3. It is not unusual for a father to look after the children while a mother is the breadwinner.

_____   _____   4. Always look for hidden motives if you are asked for help.

_____   _____   5. Every child keeps secrets from his or her parents.

_____   _____   6. Never forgive betrayal by someone you thought of as a friend.

_____   _____   7. It is a shock to realize that your grandparents will not live for ever.

_____   _____   8. Some people think too much rather than acting on ideas.

_____   _____   9. Two people can keep the same secret without knowing it.

_____   _____   10. Learning to like yourself is not always easy.

_____   _____   11. Only through a book can you step into someone else s heart and mind.

_____   _____   12. Everyone experiences moments of self-pity when feelings of abandonment take over.

ON MY HONOR

by Marion Dane Bauer, HarperCollins, 1992

Put a check on the line under AGREE if you agree with the statement. Put a check on the line under DISAGREE if you disagree with the statement.

AGREE   DISAGREE

_____   _____   1. When one of your friends rarely wants to do what your other friends want, drop the friend.

_____   _____   2. It is possible to ask a parent for permission and hope that you won't get it.

_____   _____   3. Having a friend who is a daredevil may get you into trouble.

_____   _____   4. It is never right to give or to accept a dare.

_____   _____   5. It is natural to deny that terrible things happen.

_____   _____   6. There are times when it is not possible to make things right.

_____   _____   7. Being on your honor means that a lot of trust is involved.

_____   _____   8. One lie almost invariably leads to another.

_____   _____   9. A guilty secret is impossible to live with.

_____   _____   10. Fears can be real or imagined.

_____   _____   11. Good can come out of tragedy.

_____   _____   12. Living your life by "maybes" is impossible.

ON THE FAR SIDE OF THE MOUNTAIN

by Jean Craighead George, E. P. Dutton, 1990

Put a check on the line under AGREE if you agree with the statement. Put a check on the line under DISAGREE if you disagree with the statement.

AGREE   DISAGREE

______   ______   1. Living in the wilderness is far safer than living in a big city.

______   ______   2. Every human being needs someone to talk to.

______   ______   3. Only those things natural to the woods are needed for human survival.

______   ______   4. It is easy to be deceived by one who appears to be an officer of the law.

______   ______   5. It is extremely difficult to track a person in the woods.

______   ______   6. Falcons are rare birds and worth a lot of money.

______   ______   7. One should never take a baby bird from its nest.

______   ______   8. Wild birds belong in the wild and should never be sold as pets.

______   ______   9. Some people never feel at home in a natural setting.

______   ______   10. Sometimes the greatest love means giving up the thing you love.

______   ______   11. In preserving the environment, a person who is not part of the solution is part of the problem.

______   ______   12. Every human being has a responsibility to take care of the planet Earth, which we all call home.

ONE-EYED CAT

by Paula Fox, Bradbury, 1984

Put a check on the line under AGREE if you agree with the statement. Put a check on the line under DISAGREE if you disagree with the statement.

AGREE   DISAGREE

______   ______   1. Ministers' children are expected to be role models for others.

______   ______   2. Once trust is broken it can never again be earned.

______   ______   3. Something that is forbidden is more tempting than something that is allowed.

______   ______   4. Wearing your heart on your sleeve leaves you hollow inside.

______   ______   5. Forbidden fruit can quickly turn sour.

______   ______   6. A kind person may have a cruel tongue.

______   ______   7. Superstitious people are those with little education.

______   ______   8. Nearly everything you touch is history.

______   ______   9. Hearing an old person share memories is boring.

______   ______   10. If you wait long enough, a good person will confess to any wrongdoing.

______   ______   11. Guilt is having a burden to bear for any length of time.

______   ______   12. "To thine own self be true" is the best advice a person can receive.

ORDINARY JACK: BEING THE FIRST PART
OF THE BAGTHORPE SAGA

by Helen Cresswell, Macmillan, 1977

Put a check on the line under AGREE if you agree with the statement. Put a check on the line under DISAGREE if you disagree with the statement.

AGREE   DISAGREE

1. A person who writes a newspaper advice column has no family problems.

2. Every large family has at least one child who is a misfit.

3. Some people with hearing problems pretend to be more deaf than they really are.

4. No matter what some children accomplish, their brothers and sisters will accomplish more.

5. Some people s lives are a series of failures, no matter how hard they try.

6. Fireworks should be banned because they are dangerous.

7. An exercise program should be started only with proper training.

8. A vain person is an unhappy person.

9. Anyone who claims to be able to foretell the future is a fraud.

10. Everyone is born with a special gift or talent that needs to be developed.

11. Pretending to be something you are not can only lead to disappointment.

12. No problem is too large for a loving family to solve.

ORVIS

by H. M. Hoover, Viking, 1987

Put a check on the line under AGREE if you agree with the statement. Put a check on the line under DISAGREE if you disagree with the statement.

AGREE   DISAGREE

_______   _______   1. A childhood spent in a variety of places results in a confused, mixed-up child.

_______   _______   2. People are lonely only because they choose to be.

_______   _______   3. To keep the Earth from ecological disaster, many people should be sent to other planets to live.

_______   _______   4. Children should be expected to follow the profession of their parents.

_______   _______   5. People of unusual appearance are generally treated as social outcasts.

_______   _______   6. Technology, unlike nature, quickly becomes obsolete.

_______   _______   7. Measures to extend life to 150 years or more are highly desirable.

_______   _______   8. Everyone wants to appear younger than his or her actual age.

_______   _______   9. Robots of the future can be programmed with dangerous thoughts and wreak disaster on the Earth.

_______   _______   10. Most senior citizens cannot be productive in retirement.

_______   _______   11. One must have a course in survival skills in order to survive in the wilderness.

_______   _______   12. The pioneers, who depended on nature for the basics of life, had better lives than the modern person, who depends on technology.

OUT OF THE DUST

by Karen Hesse, Scholastic, 1998

Put a check on the line under AGREE if you agree with the statement. Put a check on the line under DISAGREE if you disagree with the statement.

AGREE   DISAGREE

______   ______   1. Everyone was poor during the Great Depression.

______   ______   2. Among the poorest people in the Depression were those who lived in the dust bowl of Oklahoma.

______   ______   3. Remaining in a place where you cannot make a living shows that you don't really want to work.

______   ______   4. It is easy to mistake kerosene for water.

______   ______   5. The death of a loved one causes feelings of guilt in those left behind.

______   ______   6. Music can bring comfort to a grieving person.

______   ______   7. Surrendering to grief is the highest form of self-pity.

______   ______   8. Spending time with friends makes it possible to ignore miserable surroundings.

______   ______   9. When a parent can't be depended on, children must accept responsibility for providing food and shelter.

______   ______   10. Nightmares are grounded in a person s fears.

______   ______   11. A place of dust, wind, and dying crops would be a poor setting for a story.

______   ______   12. Every person has a talent that should be nurtured.

A PARADISE CALLED TEXAS

by Janice Jordan Shefelman, Eakin Press, 1983

Put a check on the line under AGREE if you agree with the statement. Put a check on the line under DISAGREE if you disagree with the statement.

AGREE   DISAGREE

_____   _____   1. When a stranger comes to a small town, he or she should be avoided.

_____   _____   2. No one would want to leave a comfortable home to live in the wilderness.

_____   _____   3. It is never wise to look back at your earlier life.

_____   _____   4. When a ship begins to toss and turn in a storm, the safest place to be is on deck.

_____   _____   5. It is impossible to be brave if you are afraid.

_____   _____   6. When many people are confined on a small ship, conflict is inevitable.

_____   _____   7. If it were possible to fly like a seagull, most people would want wings.

_____   _____   8. A small village may disappear without a trace.

_____   _____   9. Overcoming great hardships can make a person stronger in both mind and body.

_____   _____   10. You cannot have a school without a school building.

_____   _____   11. An illness cannot be cured without medicine.

_____   _____   12. A good time to be stubborn is when you know you are right.

PARK'S QUEST

by Katherine Paterson, E. P. Dutton, 1988

Put a check on the line under AGREE if you agree with the statement. Put a check on the line under DISAGREE if you disagree with the statement.

AGREE   DISAGREE

_____   _____   1. Family secrets are often kept from the children of the family.

_____   _____   2. Make-believe games are a waste of time.

_____   _____   3. It is important for a child to learn about a deceased parent.

_____   _____   4. Visiting relatives you have never met might lead to surprises.

_____   _____   5. A bleak welcome makes one want to go home.

_____   _____   6. It is possible to take an instant dislike to someone.

_____   _____   7. A city boy might get into trouble on a farm.

_____   _____   8. Curiosity may be dangerous.

_____   _____   9. Catching a bear cub is not a good idea.

_____   _____   10. Being a captive and being protected may be the same thing.

_____   _____   11. Running away from trouble will not solve the problem.

_____   _____   12. The books we read influence our thinking.

THE PHANTOM TOLLBOOTH

by Norton Juster, Random House, 1961

Put a check on the line under AGREE if you agree with the statement. Put a check on the line under DISAGREE if you disagree with the statement.

AGREE   DISAGREE

———   ———   1. Seeking knowledge is always a good thing.

———   ———   2. If thinking became unlawful, people would stop doing it.

———   ———   3. To get out of the doldrums, take a walk.

———   ———   4. Being on time is very important.

———   ———   5. Someone who pretends to be another person is a fraud.

———   ———   6. One should never take advice from strangers.

———   ———   7. When two sides can't agree, they must compromise.

———   ———   8. Proverbs are good rules for living.

———   ———   9. People see the same things in different ways.

———   ———   10. A world without numbers would come to a halt.

———   ———   11. Knowledge and wisdom are not the same thing.

———   ———   12. It is possible to be numb with grief.

PHOENIX RISING

by Karen Hesse, Henry Holt, 1994

Put a check on the line under AGREE if you agree with the statement. Put a check on the line under DISAGREE if you disagree with the statement.

AGREE   DISAGREE

_____   _____   1. A nuclear accident can turn a state, province, or country into a wasteland.

_____   _____   2. Some houses contain rooms in which only terrible things happen.

_____   _____   3. If you don't let anyone into your heart you will never be hurt.

_____   _____   4. A dog that attacks sheep or other farm animals should be killed.

_____   _____   5. Refugees from a disaster are rarely welcome in other towns, because they come with very little and expect charity.

_____   _____   6. Keeping a secret is impossible when others suspect that something they should know about is going on.

_____   _____   7. It is not necessary to be polite and accept a present you don't like.

_____   _____   8. Many well-educated people have had only a grade-school education.

_____   _____   9. The only thing certain in life is change.

_____   _____   10. Not sharing a secret with your best friend can break up the friendship.

_____   _____   11. Only a bully would beat up a person too weak to fight back.

_____   _____   12. Live each day to the fullest, for you never know what tomorrow will bring.

PICTURES OF HOLLIS WOODS

by Patricia Reilly Giff, Wendy Lamb Books, 2002

Put a check on the line under AGREE if you agree with the statement. Put a check on the line under DISAGREE if you disagree with the statement.

AGREE   DISAGREE

_____   _____   1. A child who is a mountain of trouble is an unhappy child.

_____   _____   2. To lead a happy life, a person must feel needed by others.

_____   _____   3. It is foolish to live with guilt about past events that cannot be changed.

_____   _____   4. The most important part of any friendship is loyalty.

_____   _____   5. A teenager would not wish to spend time with an elderly person.

_____   _____   6. Some children never have one place to call home.

_____   _____   7. It is easier to express strong feelings in art than in literature.

_____   _____   8. All older people are forgetful, and they should not live alone.

_____   _____   9. Sometimes, running away is the best way to solve a problem.

_____   _____   10. There is a difference between being needed and being wanted.

_____   _____   11. Truth is not always evident; you have to keep looking for it.

_____   _____   12. Some teenagers are their own worst enemies.

THE PINBALLS

by Betsy Byars, HarperCollins, 1977

Put a check on the line under AGREE if you agree with the statement. Put a check on the line under DISAGREE if you disagree with the statement.

AGREE   DISAGREE

______   ______   1. Not belonging to a family is a painful experience.

______   ______   2. Some people have no control over their lives.

______   ______   3. A broken promise can be very upsetting.

______   ______   4. A person with a chip on the shoulder has been hurt by someone else.

______   ______   5. A pinball machine is like life, because you never know what will happen next.

______   ______   6. Being rude to a kind person is unforgivable.

______   ______   7. Forgetting something important may cause trouble.

______   ______   8. Sometimes it is necessary to bend the rules.

______   ______   9. Some people are uncomfortable when praised.

______   ______   10. People who take action have control over their lives.

______   ______   11. To cheer someone up, give him or her a puppy.

______   ______   12. Children can gain strength from each other.

PIPPI LONGSTOCKING

by Astrid Lindgen, Random House, 1961

Put a check on the line under AGREE if you agree with the statement. Put a check on the line under DISAGREE if you disagree with the statement.

AGREE   DISAGREE

_____   _____   1. Children who live without adults can get into trouble.

_____   _____   2. Playing tag with the police is not a good idea.

_____   _____   3. Being the new girl at school can be a lot of fun.

_____   _____   4. Everyone should have a secret hiding place.

_____   _____   5. If you meet a bull while you are on a picnic, reach out and pet it.

_____   _____   6. Everyone should have and use party manners.

_____   _____   7. Being unconventional can get you into trouble.

_____   _____   8. People tend to avoid those who dress and speak differently.

_____   _____   9. A monkey and a horse make good pets.

_____   _____   10. If thieves awaken you in the middle of the night, teach them to dance.

_____   _____   11. Horses have definite likes and dislikes.

_____   _____   12. You cannot learn anything from a fantasy tale.

THE PLANET OF JUNIOR BROWN

by Virginia Hamilton, Simon & Schuster, 1971

Put a check on the line under AGREE if you agree with the statement. Put a check on the line under DISAGREE if you disagree with the statement.

AGREE   DISAGREE

_______   _______   1. As much knowledge can be gained outside a classroom as inside a classroom.

_______   _______   2. A teacher who leaves the profession will always continue to teach.

_______   _______   3. A parent who overfeeds an obese child is guilty of child abuse.

_______   _______   4. A person who lives in a fantasy world is afraid to face the real world.

_______   _______   5. A talented musician without access to a musical instrument will find a way to develop his or her talent.

_______   _______   6. Everyone wants to feel needed by another person.

_______   _______   7. Large city schools are not equipped to deal with students who are mentally or physically different.

_______   _______   8. A very dark place may be comforting rather than frightening.

_______   _______   9. It is possible to play music that no one else can hear.

_______   _______   10. Life for many people is mere survival.

_______   _______   11. Sometimes running away is the best solution to a problem.

_______   _______   12. Poor people have little hope of a better future.

THE PUSHCART WAR

by Jean Merrill, Harper & Row, 1964

Put a check on the line under AGREE if you agree with the statement. Put a check on the line under DISAGREE if you disagree with the statement.

AGREE   DISAGREE

_____   _____   1. Competition between businesses keeps prices down.

_____   _____   2. Trucks cause more traffic jams and accidents than cars do.

_____   _____   3. Trucks should be banned from big cities.

_____   _____   4. Small-business owners often help each other.

_____   _____   5. A small business can't compete against a big business that sells the same products.

_____   _____   6. Pushcart peddlers should be banned from city streets.

_____   _____   7. Protest marches can be very effective.

_____   _____   8. The best way for a citizen to make his or her views known is by writing a letter to the editor of the local newspaper.

_____   _____   9. People can be effective when they work together to solve a problem.

_____   _____   10. Shooting tacks into truck tires is not a good idea.

_____   _____   11. Sometimes famous people are interviewed on topics they know nothing about.

_____   _____   12. Right always wins in the end.

RABBIT HILL

by Robert Lawson, Viking, 1944

Put a check on the line under AGREE if you agree with the statement. Put a check on the line under DISAGREE if you disagree with the statement.

AGREE   DISAGREE

_______   _______   1. Wildlife is being destroyed by expanding towns.

_______   _______   2. New people moving into a neighborhood can be a very good thing.

_______   _______   3. Mothers often worry needlessly about their children.

_______   _______   4. Automobile accidents happen when drivers are careless.

_______   _______   5. News travels faster in the country than in the city.

_______   _______   6. Sharing with others is foolish when there is not enough to go around.

_______   _______   7. Moving to a new place can be exciting.

_______   _______   8. Children who don't listen to their parents may end up with injuries.

_______   _______   9. Dogs and woodchucks don't get along.

_______   _______   10. Ignoring a warning is asking for trouble.

_______   _______   11. If you find an injured animal, you should try to heal it.

_______   _______   12. Everyone should be concerned about protecting wildlife.

RABBLE STARKEY

by Lois Lowry, Houghton Mifflin, 1987

Put a check on the line under AGREE if you agree with the statement. Put a check on the line under DISAGREE if you disagree with the statement.

AGREE   DISAGREE

_______   _______   1. No one wants a younger brother tagging along on his or her adventures.

_______   _______   2. Some people reject any offer of kindness.

_______   _______   3. News spreads far more quickly in a small town than in a big city.

_______   _______   4. A bully is a person with little self-esteem.

_______   _______   5. Blackmail is always wrong, even if the motives for it are good.

_______   _______   6. One cannot forgive a person who has injured a friend.

_______   _______   7. Jealousy can destroy the strongest of friendships.

_______   _______   8. Self-confidence is essential in achieving any goal.

_______   _______   9. One often feels apprehensive about change, no matter how positive.

_______   _______   10. There is more than one kind of love.

_______   _______   11. Mental illness can affect other family members as well as the one who is ill.

_______   _______   12. The only thing certain about human life is change.

RASCAL

by Sterling North, E. P. Dutton, 1963

Put a check on the line under AGREE if you agree with the statement. Put a check on the line under DISAGREE if you disagree with the statement.

AGREE   DISAGREE

_______   _______   1. It would be more fun to have a raccoon than a dog for a pet.

_______   _______   2. It is impossible to make a pet out of a wild animal.

_______   _______   3. People are responsible for the damage their pets do.

_______   _______   4. If you come upon a flock of ducks, it's best to leave them alone.

_______   _______   5. An animal that destroys property should be destroyed.

_______   _______   6. It is essential to censor letters from soldiers in wartime.

_______   _______   7. People who are cruel to animals should be put in jail.

_______   _______   8. Cutting down trees without replanting can destroy the Earth.

_______   _______   9. Earning money is difficult in a rural community.

_______   _______   10. An injured wild animal should be released back into the woods when it is healed.

_______   _______   11. A flu epidemic can wipe out an entire town.

_______   _______   12. A crop can be damaged by weather, blight, and wild animals.

RASCO AND THE RATS OF NIMH

by Jane Leslie Conly, HarperCollins, 1986

Put a check on the line under AGREE if you agree with the statement. Put a check on the line under DISAGREE if you disagree with the statement.

AGREE   DISAGREE

——————   ——————   1. A poor education means few opportunities in life.

——————   ——————   2. The best thing about living in a city is the noise.

——————   ——————   3. A good friend is a treasure more precious than gold.

——————   ——————   4. People who are very different from others often achieve things the ordinary person cannot achieve.

——————   ——————   5. There are civilizations in existence that we know nothing about.

——————   ——————   6. The most important quality of a leader is the ability to listen to those who are being led.

——————   ——————   7. A surprise may be good or bad but is usually good.

——————   ——————   8. There are times when even the most carefully made plans have to be discarded.

——————   ——————   9. A monument is a good way to remember a brave person.

——————   ——————   10. Wherever dams are built, wildlife suffers.

——————   ——————   11. City people who move to the country find that they don't fit in.

——————   ——————   12. Many animals are highly intelligent.

REDWALL

by Brian Jacques, Philomel Books, 1986

Put a check on the line under AGREE if you agree with the statement. Put a check on the line under DISAGREE if you disagree with the statement.

AGREE   DISAGREE

_____   _____   1. A pacifist is a person who refuses to fight for any reason.

_____   _____   2. Ignoring obvious signs of danger is sometimes the best thing to do.

_____   _____   3. Records of past history can give direction for the future.

_____   _____   4. Fear is the most powerful weapon of all.

_____   _____   5. Warnings that appear in a dream should be taken seriously.

_____   _____   6. Soldiers who are brave and strong never weep.

_____   _____   7. Overconfidence may lead to defeat.

_____   _____   8. Strength in numbers can be offset by cunning and trickery.

_____   _____   9. An enemy should be treated with kindness.

_____   _____   10. Being completely at the mercy of a captor is devastating.

_____   _____   11. To achieve victory, slow and methodical is often better than brave and daring.

_____   _____   12. A person with no compassion would not be expected to keep his or her word.

THE REMARKABLE JOURNEY OF PRINCE JEN

by Lloyd Alexander, E. P. Dutton, 1991

Put a check on the line under AGREE if you agree with the statement. Put a check on the line under DISAGREE if you disagree with the statement.

AGREE   DISAGREE

______   ______   1. A country in which all the people live in happiness and harmony could not possibly exist.

______   ______   2. Most people would help someone in obvious need, even it it meant going out of their way to do so.

______   ______   3. If one has a natural gift for music, it should be nurtured even if the cost is great.

______   ______   4. Magical objects can appear only in fantasy tales.

______   ______   5. It is foolish to put your life in danger to help a stranger.

______   ______   6. Life without the one you love is meaningless.

______   ______   7. Being a king is meaningless if you cannot prove that you are a king.

______   ______   8. Only a very careless person would lose gifts intended for others.

______   ______   9. In real life, it is not possible to put a spell on someone.

______   ______   10. All of us have wasted time in useless pursuits.

______   ______   11. People often have what they seek and don't realize it.

______   ______   12. Self-doubt is a person s greatest enemy.

THE REPTILE ROOM

by Lemony Snicket, HarperCollins, 1999

Put a check on the line under AGREE if you agree with the statement. Put a check on the line under DISAGREE if you disagree with the statement.

AGREE   DISAGREE

_______   _______   1. For most people, life is a series of misfortunes.

_______   _______   2. A lawn with hedges shaped like snakes would be a dangerous place to explore.

_______   _______   3. All snakes are poisonous and should be avoided.

_______   _______   4. A room full of snakes would be a fun place to visit.

_______   _______   5. When adults will not listen to you, yell louder.

_______   _______   6. A premonition of danger should be heeded.

_______   _______   7. Often people who mean well cause a lot of damage.

_______   _______   8. A herpetologist studies all kinds of strange birds.

_______   _______   9. A person caught in a lie should tell the truth.

_______   _______   10. A person caught in a lie should keep still and say nothing.

_______   _______   11. Two people may study the same data but arrive at different conclusions.

_______   _______   12. Life is a series of unfortunate events.

RETURN OF THE INDIAN

by Lynne Reid Banks, Doubleday, 1986

Put a check on the line under AGREE if you agree with the statement. Put a check on the line under DISAGREE if you disagree with the statement.

AGREE   DISAGREE

_______   _______   1. Moving to a new neighborhood can be a great adventure.

_______   _______   2. A triumph is not complete until it is shared.

_______   _______   3. It is okay to refuse when you are asked to help and don't know what to do.

_______   _______   4. Not wanting to face the truth is a sign of cowardice.

_______   _______   5. Borrowing something without permission is the same as stealing.

_______   _______   6. It is difficult to conceal your feelings.

_______   _______   7. War hurts innocent people, not just those who are fighting.

_______   _______   8. When cultures clash, war is inevitable.

_______   _______   9. When one has the voice of authority, people listen.

_______   _______   10. The qualities of a leader are hard to define.

_______   _______   11. Rushing into a new situation can be rewarding.

_______   _______   12. When all the odds are against you, it is wise to give up.

RIFLES FOR WATIE

by Harold Keith, Crowell, 1957

Put a check on the line under AGREE if you agree with the statement. Put a check on the line under DISAGREE if you disagree with the statement.

AGREE   DISAGREE

_____   _____   1. A prolonged drought can destroy an entire crop.

_____   _____   2. A new recruit in the army might feel excited and lost at the same time.

_____   _____   3. It is your duty to stop a friend who is heading for big trouble.

_____   _____   4. The feeling in a town just before a big battle is apprehension.

_____   _____   5. Farmers do not do well with land that is two rocks to one dirt.

_____   _____   6. When a person is starving, stealing food is not a crime.

_____   _____   7. A Union scout in Rebel territory would be shot on sight.

_____   _____   8. It is wrong to deceive someone who befriends you.

_____   _____   9. In the Civil War it was possible for brothers to fight each other.

_____   _____   10. Some people enjoy watching others suffer.

_____   _____   11. A soldier who changes sides in a war is a traitor.

_____   _____   12. It is impossible to shake off a bloodhound that is on your tail.

THE RIGHTEOUS REVENGE OF ARTEMIS BONNER

by Walter Dean Myers, HarperCollins, 1992

Put a check on the line under AGREE if you agree with the statement. Put a check on the line under DISAGREE if you disagree with the statement.

AGREE   DISAGREE

_______   _______   1. Taking revenge on another person is never satisfying.

_______   _______   2. A scoundrel has no regard for people or property.

_______   _______   3. It is difficult to be brave when danger stares you in the face.

_______   _______   4. The Buffalo Soldiers of 1880 were a troop that hunted buffalo.

_______   _______   5. One should never underestimate a crack shot.

_______   _______   6. In the Old West, filing a claim for a gold mine was a long and involved process.

_______   _______   7. Depending on a mule for transportation is not a good idea.

_______   _______   8. A true friend always tells you the truth, even if you don't want to hear it.

_______   _______   9. In 1880, the streets of Tombstone, Arizona, would not have been a good place to congregate or promenade.

_______   _______   10. It is best to run from a fight if your opponent is bigger than you are.

_______   _______   11. Only real villains stoop to trickery to win a fight.

_______   _______   12. A person without "enough decency to fill a thimble" belongs in jail.

ROLL OF THUNDER, HEAR MY CRY

by Mildred Taylor, Dial, 1976

Put a check on the line under AGREE if you agree with the statement. Put a check on the line under DISAGREE if you disagree with the statement.

AGREE   DISAGREE

——— ——— 1. Maintaining pride and independence was extremely difficult for most people in the Depression years.

——— ——— 2. No child should have to use schoolbooks that are falling apart.

——— ——— 3. Night riders are cowards to be feared.

——— ——— 4. No one should lose a job after many years of faithful service, no matter what the circumstances are.

——— ——— 5. Helping a homeless person can be dangerous.

——— ——— 6. It would be better to stay home than to walk a great distance to and from school each day.

——— ——— 7. More often than not, pranks backfire on the prankster.

——— ——— 8. Getting even is not always the wise thing to do, no matter what the provocation might be.

——— ——— 9. Fighting never solves problems.

——— ——— 10. Discrimination and prejudice are the same thing.

——— ——— 11. A gift is truly meaningful when a sacrifice on the part of the giver is evident.

——— ——— 12. It is foolhardy to risk all that one owns for the good of others.

ROOTS IN THE OUTFIELD

by Jane Ziepoli, Houghton Mifflin, 1988

Put a check on the line under AGREE if you agree with the statement. Put a check on the line under DISAGREE if you disagree with the statement.

AGREE   DISAGREE

_____   _____   1. When a bat never connects with a ball, it's time to quit playing.

_____   _____   2. On every team, one person has to be the worst player.

_____   _____   3. Reading another person s letter is the same as eavesdropping.

_____   _____   4. An enemy one week can be a friend the next.

_____   _____   5. Running away will never solve a problem.

_____   _____   6. If you face your fears, you will conquer them.

_____   _____   7. Doing someone else's homework is the same as cheating on a test.

_____   _____   8. Nicknames are often meant to hurt.

_____   _____   9. First impressions are important.

_____   _____   10. It is natural to be nervous about a big game.

_____   _____   11. When a parent doesn't understand, try to explain in a different way.

_____   _____   12. The longer you are with someone without talking, the harder it is to communicate.

RUN AWAY HOME

by Patricia McKissack, Scholastic, 1997

Put a check on the line under AGREE if you agree with the statement. Put a check on the line under DISAGREE if you disagree with the statement.

AGREE   DISAGREE

_____   _____   1. When Geronimo and the Apache tribe surrendered in 1886, they were sent for two years to Florida, where many died.

_____   _____   2. Native American husbands were separated from their wives and children.

_____   _____   3. In the 1800s, it was wrong to harbor an escaped Native American.

_____   _____   4. Some secrets are impossible to keep.

_____   _____   5. It is wrong to protect an outsider if it means danger to your family.

_____   _____   6. It is possible to become jealous of someone you once liked.

_____   _____   7. A homeless person should be helped, regardless of the reason for the homelessness.

_____   _____   8. In the nineteenth century, Native Americans were justified in fighting for the land they called home.

_____   _____   9. First impressions are important.

_____   _____   10. Some organizations arise out of prejudice and bigotry.

_____   _____   11. One must do what is right, regardless of the consequences to others.

_____   _____   12. Jim Crow laws were a shameful part of American history.

SADAKO AND THE THOUSAND PAPER CRANES

by Eleanor Coerr, Putnam's, 1977

Put a check on the line under AGREE if you agree with the statement. Put a check on the line under DISAGREE if you disagree with the statement.

AGREE   DISAGREE

1. It is foolish to believe in good luck signs.

2. Most people have forgotten or ignore the purpose of a memorial day.

3. Being in a hurry to get somewhere means that you are anticipating a joyful occasion.

4. People who always want to be first are basically selfish.

5. It is true that practice makes perfect.

6. Keeping a secret is never an easy thing to do.

7. Every family will receive bad news at one time or another.

8. It is foolish to keep trying when you know you are going to lose.

9. The best way to pass lonely hours is to read.

10. Some people refuse to accept painful truths.

11. A positive attitude can help a sick person recover.

12. A statue is a fitting monument for a brave person.

SARAH BISHOP

by Scott O'Dell, Houghton Mifflin, 1980

Put a check on the line under AGREE if you agree with the statement. Put a check on the line under DISAGREE if you disagree with the statement.

AGREE   DISAGREE

_______   _______   1. Prejudice existed during the Revolutionary War period just as it exists today.

_______   _______   2. Prejudice may wear many disguises.

_______   _______   3. A ruler who does not understand the people he rules is destined to lose his throne.

_______   _______   4. Night raiders who plunder and destroy are cowards.

_______   _______   5. One will never be punished if falsely accused of a crime.

_______   _______   6. Slavery may take many forms.

_______   _______   7. "Meddling with strife that does not belong to you is like taking a dog by the ears."

_______   _______   8. Quakers did not fight for either side in the American Revolution.

_______   _______   9. Revenge may leave a bitter taste.

_______   _______   10. People throughout history have paid with their lives for their beliefs.

_______   _______   11. It is impossible to survive alone in a cave during a bitter winter.

_______   _______   12. When one has been badly treated, it is difficult to find kindness in other people.

SARAH PLAIN AND TALL

by Patricia MacLachlan, HarperCollins, 1985

Put a check on the line under AGREE if you agree with the statement. Put a check on the line under DISAGREE if you disagree with the statement.

AGREE   DISAGREE

_____   _____   1. Singing can help when you are sad or afraid.

_____   _____   2. Children raised in one-parent families can be as successful in life as children raised in two-parent families.

_____   _____   3. Someone who is loud and pesky is no fun to be around.

_____   _____   4. Meeting someone for the first time may be uncomfortable.

_____   _____   5. Ordering a bride by mail is ridiculous.

_____   _____   6. Stepmothers are usually unkind to stepchildren.

_____   _____   7. Homesickness can make one as ill as measles or the flu.

_____   _____   8. Wishing to be perfect is a waste of time.

_____   _____   9. Dogs are able to sense good and evil in people simply by looking at them.

_____   _____   10. It would be impossible to live in a house without running water.

_____   _____   11. Children should not be expected to walk three miles to school.

_____   _____   12. A house and a home are two different things.

SATURNALIA

by Paul Fleischman, HarperCollins, 1990

Put a check on the line under AGREE if you agree with the statement. Put a check on the line under DISAGREE if you disagree with the statement.

AGREE   DISAGREE

______   ______   1. Slavery in any form is to be condemned.

______   ______   2. A Native American child taken from his or her tribe will always want to return to it.

______   ______   3. People often take out their anger on those who are not responsible for their losses.

______   ______   4. To deliberately get another person into trouble is okay if you feel that the person deserves to be punished.

______   ______   5. It is foolish to help those in need at the cost of your own safety.

______   ______   6. A twin will always know when his or her twin is in trouble.

______   ______   7. Saturnalia is a feast day when servants change places with their masters.

______   ______   8. The worst thing that can happen to a person is to be unjustly accused of a terrible crime.

______   ______   9. There are times when not knowing how to read or write can save your life.

______   ______   10. It is not possible to feel love and loyalty to two totally different worlds.

______   ______   11. Those who treat others badly will one day pay for their cruelties.

______   ______   12. At times it is possible to outsmart yourself.

SAVAGE SAM

by Fred Gipson, Harper & Row, 1962

Put a check on the line under AGREE if you agree with the statement. Put a check on the line under DISAGREE if you disagree with the statement.

AGREE   DISAGREE

————   ————   1. Most people dislike a person who talks too much.

————   ————   2. A pretty girl can make a boy nervous.

————   ————   3. If dirty green water is all that is available, you should drink it.

————   ————   4. A Texas farm in the 1870s was a dangerous place to live.

————   ————   5. Trapping a bobcat down a hole is the best way to capture it.

————   ————   6. Native American captives found escape to be impossible.

————   ————   7. It is possible to ride upside down on a horse.

————   ————   8. Much more work was expected of pioneer children than of farm children today.

————   ————   9. If you bite off and swallow part of a Native American's ear, you become part Native American.

————   ————   10. Being shot by mistake hurts less than being shot deliberately.

————   ————   11. If you found a pile of horseshoes out in the middle of nowhere, you should expect to have good luck.

————   ————   12. A dog never growls at its master.

SAVE QUEEN OF SHEBA

by Louise Moeri, E. P. Dutton, 1981

Put a check on the line under AGREE if you agree with the statement. Put a check on the line under DISAGREE if you disagree with the statement.

AGREE   DISAGREE

_______   _______   1. A peaceful landscape may be the scene of terrible violence.

_______   _______   2. Pioneers on the Oregon Trail had visions of prosperity.

_______   _______   3. Older brothers should feel responsible for the safety of their younger sisters.

_______   _______   4. A cold breakfast can be as good for you as a hot breakfast.

_______   _______   5. The weather on the open prairie can change within a few minutes.

_______   _______   6. When the odds are against you, it is best to give up.

_______   _______   7. An impudent person is no fun to be around.

_______   _______   8. In a hard rain, stay away from trees.

_______   _______   9. Older brothers feel ambivalent about younger sisters.

_______   _______   10. Never begin a journey if you do not know how it will end.

_______   _______   11. Leaving a nice home in the East for an unknown home in the West is foolish.

_______   _______   12. People's first reaction to having something stolen is anger.

THE SCARECROW AND HIS SERVANT

by Philip Pullman, Alfred A. Knopf, 2005

Put a check on the line under AGREE if you agree with the statement. Put a check on the line under DISAGREE if you disagree with the statement.

AGREE   DISAGREE

______   ______   1. Factories should be built on any available land, including farmland, to make the things we need.

______   ______   2. Lightning can bring nonhuman things to life.

______   ______   3. Never argue with a brigand; give him whatever he wants.

______   ______   4. Stealing food to feed the hungry is not a crime.

______   ______   5. A hard day's work for two meals is a fair trade.

______   ______   6. The best thing to do when you are upset is to yell and scream.

______   ______   7. One who deserts a battlefield is not always a coward.

______   ______   8. If given a choice between water and jewels, most people would choose jewels.

______   ______   9. The worst place to be in a storm is in a boat on the water.

______   ______   10. No matter how far you travel, home is always the best place to be.

______   ______   11. Disputes that affect a lot of people are best settled in the courts.

______   ______   12. You cannot buy friendship; you must earn it.

THE SECRET GARDEN

by Frances Hodgson Burnett, Alfred A. Knopf, 1988

Put a check on the line under AGREE if you agree with the statement. Put a check on the line under DISAGREE if you disagree with the statement.

AGREE   DISAGREE

_______   _______   1. Unwanted children often lash out at others.

_______   _______   2. Exploring a 100-room house would be scary.

_______   _______   3. People often feel challenged to act when they are forbidden to do something.

_______   _______   4. Bad-tempered people don't like themselves.

_______   _______   5. Some people can actually talk to wild animals and be understood.

_______   _______   6. A cry in the night usually means that someone is having a bad dream.

_______   _______   7. When two stubborn people argue, a fight is inevitable.

_______   _______   8. The beauty in nature can turn to ugliness very quickly.

_______   _______   9. Many things can be accomplished through the power of positive thinking.

_______   _______   10. Some people have a green thumb, but many people don't.

_______   _______   11. Recovering from an illness is like learning to fly.

_______   _______   12. Where you tend a rose, a thistle cannot grow.

THE SECRET OF THE INDIAN

by Lynne Reid Banks, Doubleday, 1989

Put a check on the line under AGREE if you agree with the statement. Put a check on the line under DISAGREE if you disagree with the statement.

AGREE   DISAGREE

_______   _______   1. Only in a fantasy tale could inanimate objects come to life.

_______   _______   2. One who demands too much of others will end up with nothing.

_______   _______   3. It would be fascinating to become three inches tall for a short time.

_______   _______   4. Skinheads are bigoted people who belong in jail.

_______   _______   5. It is easy to make a mistake when you are dealing with magic.

_______   _______   6. Time-trekking to another time and place would be an adventure most people would want to have.

_______   _______   7. Some people are hard to get along with, and there is not much you can do about it.

_______   _______   8. Negotiation is always better than combat in settling a dispute.

_______   _______   9. The more diverse cultures learn about each other, the more likely they are to live together peacefully.

_______   _______   10. Having a variety of opinions is better than everyone believing the same thing.

_______   _______   11. A cyclone is more destructive than a hurricane.

_______   _______   12. Native Americans fought the early settlers because they had to, not because they wanted to.

THE SECRET SCHOOL

by Avi, Harcourt, 2001

Put a check on the line under AGREE if you agree with the statement. Put a check on the line under DISAGREE if you disagree with the statement.

AGREE   DISAGREE

_______   _______   1. Children in one-room schools did not learn as much as children in modern schools.

_______   _______   2. Deceiving others is a good thing to do if people benefit from the deception.

_______   _______   3. A fourteen-year-old hasn't learned enough to teach children in the elementary grades.

_______   _______   4. Silence is best if you don't agree with another's viewpoint.

_______   _______   5. Many farm families don't see the need for their children to go to high school.

_______   _______   6. It is impossible to keep a secret in a small town.

_______   _______   7. There may be good reasons for breaking a window and entering a building that is not your home.

_______   _______   8. You can't force people to learn if they choose not to.

_______   _______   9. Everyone should be able to teach, because everyone has gone to school.

_______   _______   10. Good teachers care very much about the success of their students.

_______   _______   11. Never underestimate the power of the press.

_______   _______   12. Some rules are made to be broken.

THE SERPENT NEVER SLEEPS

by Scott O'Dell, Houghton Mifflin, 1987

Put a check on the line under AGREE if you agree with the statement. Put a check on the line under DISAGREE if you disagree with the statement.

AGREE   DISAGREE

_______   _______ 1. An unexpected meeting with a king would be upsetting.

_______   _______ 2. When words are misunderstood, trouble follows.

_______   _______ 3. It is desirable to confront someone who has wronged you.

_______   _______ 4. A quarrel is best settled by a third party.

_______   _______ 5. Setting out for an unknown land is foolish.

_______   _______ 6. When a task seems overwhelming, give up.

_______   _______ 7. Conspirators always meet and work in secret.

_______   _______ 8. To plead a cause is useless when only hostile ears are listening.

_______   _______ 9. Rumors do more harm than good.

_______   _______ 10. Force won't work when it meets a strong belief.

_______   _______ 11. Choosing between food and ammunition would be difficult if you lived in a hostile wilderness.

_______   _______ 12. The Jamestown settlers would not have survived without the help of the Native Americans.

SHADES OF GRAY
by Carolyn Reeder, Macmillan, 1989

Put a check on the line under AGREE if you agree with the statement. Put a check on the line under DISAGREE if you disagree with the statement.

AGREE   DISAGREE

_______   _______ 1. A city boy will not take well to farm life.

_______   _______ 2. It is possible to survive on a diet of beans and grain.

_______   _______ 3. In any war, one side is always right and the other wrong.

_______   _______ 4. Refusing to defend your country in war means you are a coward.

_______   _______ 5. Respect must be earned.

_______   _______ 6. People are not the only enemies of humankind.

_______   _______ 7. You don't have to like a person to respect his or her beliefs.

_______   _______ 8. Sometimes, telling the truth is not the best thing to do.

_______   _______ 9. You should not ask someone for help if you don't agree with his or her beliefs.

_______   _______ 10. With no television, people 100 years ago must have been bored in the evening.

_______   _______ 11. Hard work does not always result in a job well done.

_______   _______ 12. A person who walks away from a fight knows he or she can win.

SHADOW OF A BULL

by Maia Wojciechowska, Atheneum, 1964

Put a check on the line under AGREE if you agree with the statement. Put a check on the line under DISAGREE if you disagree with the statement.

AGREE   DISAGREE

______   ______   1. Sons are expected to be like their fathers.

______   ______   2. A bullfighter cannot cheat death in the ring for ever.

______   ______   3. Famous people are remembered more for their accomplishments than for their personalities.

______   ______   4. A prophecy is the telling of an event that will actually take place in the future.

______   ______   5. One reason for showing a bull's horns is to instill fear in the bullfighter.

______   ______   6. Confidence in doing a task comes with practice.

______   ______   7. It is easy to let others make decisions for you.

______   ______   8. Keeping a promise made to oneself is more important than keeping a promise made to others.

______   ______   9. Only cowards refuse to take on dangerous jobs.

______   ______   10. The marketplace is the gossip center of every small town.

______   ______   11. It is wrong to be forced to be someone you are not.

______   ______   12. There is a difference between being foolhardy and being brave.

SHADOWS IN THE WATER

by Kathryn Lasky, Harcourt Brace Jovanovich, 1992

Put a check on the line under AGREE if you agree with the statement. Put a check on the line under DISAGREE if you disagree with the statement.

AGREE   DISAGREE

_______   _______   1. Most students are addicted to normality.

_______   _______   2. Some people can send their thoughts to others.

_______   _______   3. A military school is a place for students with discipline problems.

_______   _______   4. Poachers and polluters damage sea life through their selfish actions.

_______   _______   5. People seeking freedom will fight for it.

_______   _______   6. Dreams can reveal our future actions.

_______   _______   7. Witholding essential information may cause a disaster.

_______   _______   8. Learning to trust someone is difficult.

_______   _______   9. Every day we trust dozens of people we have never met.

_______   _______   10. If one is afraid, one cannot be brave.

_______   _______   11. When wild animals act strangely, danger is near.

_______   _______   12. It is vitally important to keep the oceans clean.

SHILOH

by Phyllis Reynolds Naylor, Macmillan, 1991

Put a check on the line under AGREE if you agree with the statement. Put a check on the line under DISAGREE if you disagree with the statement.

AGREE   DISAGREE

_______   _______   1. Hiking in the woods can be dangerous.

_______   _______   2. If someone kicked a dog, he or she should be arrested.

_______   _______   3. It is difficult for a young person who lives in a rural area to earn money.

_______   _______   4. Telling a lie is sometimes the best thing to do.

_______   _______   5. A person should not keep secrets from his or her family.

_______   _______   6. Getting caught in a lie is embarrassing.

_______   _______   7. It is foolish to want another s possessions.

_______   _______   8. Stray dogs should be shot before they become rabid.

_______   _______   9. It is right to hide an animal if you know the owner mistreats it.

_______   _______   10. A pet is a luxury that poor people can't afford.

_______   _______   11. Laws are written to protect animals as well as people.

_______   _______   12. Not telling the whole truth is the same as lying.

SHOEBAG

by Mary James (M. E. Kerr), Scholastic, 1990

Put a check on the line under AGREE if you agree with the statement. Put a check on the line under DISAGREE if you disagree with the statement.

AGREE   DISAGREE

______   ______   1. Roaches are nocturnal creatures that should be destroyed on sight.

______   ______   2. All food should be kept either hot or cold and never left out for long periods of time.

______   ______   3. Children who lead sheltered lives will not be able to cope with life as adults.

______   ______   4. In the absence of innate talent, fame in the entertainment field disappears with aging.

______   ______   5. The first day in a new school is always traumatic.

______   ______   6. A bully is a coward with little self-esteem.

______   ______   7. Children make fun of those who look or dress differently.

______   ______   8. Every school has a group of social misfits or outcasts.

______   ______   9. Human beings operate according to double standards when it comes to wildlife.

______   ______   10. Few people see themselves or others as they really are.

______   ______   11. Some good arises from every disaster.

______   ______   12. It is a rare human being who can always keep a promise.

SHOESHINE GIRL

by Clyde Robert Bulla, Crowell, 1975

Put a check on the line under AGREE if you agree with the statement. Put a check on the line under DISAGREE if you disagree with the statement.

AGREE   DISAGREE

______   ______   1. Some people steal just for kicks, not because they can't pay for what they have stolen.

______   ______   2. Money in your pocket means independence.

______   ______   3. Most parents would object to a ten-year-old taking a paying job.

______   ______   4. Shoplifting is a crime that should result in a jail sentence.

______   ______   5. Borrowing on your allowance is not a good idea.

______   ______   6. Children should be allowed to choose their own friends.

______   ______   7. It is easy to lose your temper when people don't see things your way.

______   ______   8. It is not always necessaary to tell adults where you are going.

______   ______   9. It is harder to spend money you earn than to spend money that was a gift.

______   ______   10. Helping people feel better makes the helper feel better.

______   ______   11. Making fun of something a person takes pride in is cruel.

______   ______   12. Riding alone on a train is an exciting adventure.

SIDEWAYS STORIES FROM WAYSIDE SCHOOL

by Louis Sachar, William Morrow, 1998

Put a check on the line under AGREE if you agree with the statement. Put a check on the line under DISAGREE if you disagree with the statement.

AGREE   DISAGREE

_______   _______   1. Only a foolish student would challenge a mean teacher.

_______   _______   2. It is possible to get the right answers in math and not know how you arrived at the answers.

_______   _______   3. Some people can't help being non stop talkers.

_______   _______   4. Teachers often ask students to do the impossible.

_______   _______   5. The most important job of a class president is to listen.

_______   _______   6. Negative people never change.

_______   _______   7. It is easier to give in than to resist temptation.

_______   _______   8. Second graders look cute without their front teeth.

_______   _______   9. New students rarely receive a warm welcome in a school.

_______   _______   10. A smile can be catching.

_______   _______   11. There is never a good reason for hating everybody.

_______   _______   12. It is possible to enjoy playing a game even though you are no good at it.

SIGN OF THE BEAVER

by Elizabeth George Speare, Houghton Mifflin, 1983

Put a check on the line under AGREE if you agree with the statement. Put a check on the line under DISAGREE if you disagree with the statement.

AGREE   DISAGREE

______   ______   1. A careless act may be life threatening.

______   ______   2. Trust must be earned.

______   ______   3. A twelve-year-old can survive alone in the wilderness for months.

______   ______   4. The most essential wilderness survival skill is hunting.

______   ______   5. Learning to read was an essential skill in early America.

______   ______   6. It is difficult for people of different backgrounds to become friends.

______   ______   7. In the eighteenth century, Native Americans believed that no one could own land.

______   ______   8. When local customs differ from yours, ignore them.

______   ______   9. To be accepted into a new group, one needs to adopt its customs.

______   ______   10. One cannot have friendship without respect.

______   ______   11. Gambling nearly always leads to trouble.

______   ______   12. One way to teach reading to a reluctant reader is to read aloud to that person.

SING DOWN THE MOON

by Scott O'Dell, Houghton Mifflin, 1970

Put a check on the line under AGREE if you agree with the statement. Put a check on the line under DISAGREE if you disagree with the statement.

AGREE   DISAGREE

_______   _______   1. Freedom is usually taken for granted by those who have it.

_______   _______   2. The older you become, the more difficult it is to learn another language.

_______   _______   3. Sometimes it is hard to know whom to trust.

_______   _______   4. Because goods were scarce, settlers never stole from each other.

_______   _______   5. Learning to read was an essential skill in early America.

_______   _______   6. It is difficult for people of different backgrounds to become friends.

_______   _______   7. In the eighteenth century, Native Americans believed that no one could own land.

_______   _______   8. When local customs differ from yours, ignore them.

_______   _______   9. To be accepted into a new group, one needs to adopt its customs.

_______   _______   10. One cannot have friendship without respect.

_______   _______   11. Gambling nearly always leads to trouble.

_______   _______   12. One way to teach reading to a reluctant reader is to read aloud to that person.

A SINGLE SHARD

by Linda Sue Park, Houghton Mifflin, 2001

Put a check on the line under AGREE if you agree with the statement. Put a check on the line under DISAGREE if you disagree with the statement.

AGREE   DISAGREE

______   ______   1. Two homeless people staying together are more likely to survive than one homeless person living alone.

______   ______   2. There is much the young can learn from the old.

______   ______   3. A teacher who never praises anyone will have pupils who stop trying.

______   ______   4. Scholars read the great words of the world, but the homeless must learn to read the world itself.

______   ______   5. Talent will produce nothing without hard work.

______   ______   6. If no one knows you have damaged another s property, you still must pay for the damage.

______   ______   7. If you discover that a competitor has a better way of producing goods, you should share the competitor's secret with your employer.

______   ______   8. Every human being has a special talent or passion that should be developed.

______   ______   9. Often it takes courage to choose life over death.

______   ______   10. Work gives a person dignity. Stealing takes it away.

______   ______   11. Quite often, a good deed balances a bad one.

______   ______   12. The wind that blows one door shut often blows another door open.

SIXTH-GRADE SLEEPOVER

by Eve Bunting, Harcourt Brace Jovanovich, 1986

Put a check on the line under AGREE if you agree with the statement. Put a check on the line under DISAGREE if you disagree with the statement.

AGREE   DISAGREE

______   ______   1. Some secrets are better shared.

______   ______   2. Big problems become bigger if you keep them hidden.

______   ______   3. Always expect the unexpected.

______   ______   4. Many people hide the fact that they cannot read.

______   ______   5. Fear of the dark is irrational and easy to overcome.

______   ______   6. Don't ask for favors if you are not prepared to return them.

______   ______   7. You don't have to read the book to write a book report.

______   ______   8. A really true friend will keep your secrets.

______   ______   9. It is never acceptable to twist the truth.

______   ______   10. The best way to accomplish a task is to begin it.

______   ______   11. It is better to face fears than to ignore them.

______   ______   12. Class clowns show off because they get no attention at home.

SKINNYBONES

by Barbara Park, Alfred A. Knopf, 1982

Put a check on the line under AGREE if you agree with the statement. Put a check on the line under DISAGREE if you disagree with the statement.

AGREE   DISAGREE

______   ______   1. The odds against winning a national contest are very high.

______   ______   2. The most popular student is the class clown.

______   ______   3. Teachers don't appreciate students who talk back.

______   ______   4. One way to make friends is to be a friend.

______   ______   5. Receiving a sports award is always thrilling.

______   ______   6. No one cheers for a team that is always in last place.

______   ______   7. Claiming a talent one doesn't have is foolish.

______   ______   8. It is easy to find ways to waste time.

______   ______   9. It is hard to sleep the night before a big game.

______   ______   10. Losing a game doesn't matter if you play well.

______   ______   11. When you know you are right, it is time to disagree with the umpire.

______   ______   12. Running away from a problem is wise when you don't know how to solve it.

SKYLARK

by Patricia MacLachlan, HarperCollins, 1994

Put a check on the line under AGREE if you agree with the statement. Put a check on the line under DISAGREE if you disagree with the statement.

AGREE   DISAGREE

_____   _____   1. The one thing farmers fear most is drought.

_____   _____   2. When a family falls upon hard times, family members should stick together.

_____   _____   3. No one would deliberately hurt another's feelings.

_____   _____   4. Some fathers treat their children as if they do not exist.

_____   _____   5. When a pioneer child had free time, he or she was allowed to play.

_____   _____   6. When a river runs dry, settlers have to move on.

_____   _____   7. A coyote is dangerous to farm animals.

_____   _____   8. Pioneer life brought many hardships but also many joys.

_____   _____   9. A farmer who faces a drought should give up and find another way to make a living.

_____   _____   10. Homesickness can be cured only by going home.

_____   _____   11. No problem is too big to be solved with thought and effort.

_____   _____   12. Pioneers who went West had no idea of the hardships they would face.

SLAVE DANCER

by Paula Fox, Bradbury, 1973

Put a check on the line under AGREE if you agree with the statement. Put a check on the line under DISAGREE if you disagree with the statement.

AGREE   DISAGREE

_____   _____   1. Parents always know what is best for their children.

_____   _____   2. Someone who appears to be kind may really be an enemy.

_____   _____   3. Moonlight is not always comforting.

_____   _____   4. One may feel lonely when surrounded by many others.

_____   _____   5. Sometimes, doing illegal deeds is acceptable.

_____   _____   6. The truth doesn't matter when one is powerless.

_____   _____   7. At one time in history, human beings were treated as merchandise.

_____   _____   8. Hating someone can be a frightening feeling.

_____   _____   9. Memories of a journey are not always pleasant.

_____   _____   10. Something that brings pleasure may also bring pain.

_____   _____   11. A person who cannot carry a tune is unable to enjoy music.

_____   _____   12. When a person changes, it is usually for the better.

SMALL STEPS

by Louis Sachar, Delacorte, 2006.

Put a check on the line under AGREE if you agree with the statement. ut a check on the line under DISAGREE if you disagree with the statement.

AGREE   DISAGREE

_____   _____   1. One should not associate with a person who has served a prison sentence.

_____   _____   2. It is impossible to do the right thing when everyone expects the worst from you.

_____   _____   3. A basket of popcorn can send someone to prison.

_____   _____   4. One should envy the life of a female rock star.

_____   _____   5. It is best to avoid "get rich quick" schemes.

_____   _____   6. It is wise to watch your tongue in front of a teacher or coach.

_____   _____   7. Some people have poor taste in clothes and don't know it.

_____   _____   8. If someone tries to control you, the best thing to do is run away.

_____   _____   9. Only unbalanced people have tattoos and pierced tongues.

_____   _____   10. Not all seizures can be blamed on drug overdose.

_____   _____   11. A rock singer doesn't have to know the words if he or she can simply make a lot of noise.

_____   _____   12. When two people want the same thing, the smarter person usually wins over the stronger person.

SNAP: A NOVEL

by Allison McGhee, Candlewick, 2004

Put a check on the line under AGREE if you agree with the statement. Put a check on the line under DISAGREE if you disagree with the statement.

AGREE   DISAGREE

——— ——— 1. Making lists ensures a well-ordered life.

——— ——— 2. Snapping a rubber band on your wrist can cure you of a bad habit.

——— ——— 3. It is possible to care deeply for a person yet say hurtful things to that person.

——— ——— 4. People have hidden lives; they are not what they seem to be.

——— ——— 5. People who refuse to talk do so because they have nothing to say.

——— ——— 6. Everyone would be healthier if there were no sugar.

——— ——— 7. A shack to one person may be a home to another.

——— ——— 8. It is best not to care deeply about someone, since you will one day lose that person.

——— ——— 9. No matter how difficult it is, people always find ways to cope with the world.

——— ——— 10. You can always tell when someone is keeping something from you.

——— ——— 11. You cannot force people to take on a responsibility that is rightfully theirs.

——— ——— 12. Refusing to face life and its problems is a form of self-pity.

SNOW TREASURE

by Marie McSwigan, Scholastic, 1958

Put a check on the line under AGREE if you agree with the statement. Put a check on the line under DISAGREE if you disagree with the statement.

AGREE   DISAGREE

_______   _______   1. A long winter with a good amount of snow means children's days will be filled with fun.

_______   _______   2. Parents worry when children arrive home late from school.

_______   _______   3. Many parents trust children to perform adult tasks.

_______   _______   4. Sometimes a familiar place becomes unfamiliar.

_______   _______   5. Learning something new under stressful conditions is difficult.

_______   _______   6. Negative events in people's lives are caused by bad luck.

_______   _______   7. Ignoring a curfew can be very dangerous.

_______   _______   8. No matter how much people have, they usually want more.

_______   _______   9. A feeling of being watched is comforting.

_______   _______   10. A story that sounds true probably is true.

_______   _______   11. Sometimes trouble is unavoidable.

_______   _______   12. There have always been wars and there will always be wars, regardless of people's efforts to avoid them.

SOS TITANIC

by Eve Bunting, Harcourt, Brace, 1996

Put a check on the line under AGREE if you agree with the statement. Put a check on the line under DISAGREE if you disagree with the statement.

AGREE   DISAGREE

_______   _______   1. Parents often have good reasons to leave their children in the care of others.

_______   _______   2. There may be many omens of disaster before disaster strikes.

_______   _______   3. A bully is a person with low self-esteem.

_______   _______   4. A child should not be expected to make a long ocean voyage alone.

_______   _______   5. The best age for a child to be sent off to boarding school is age eight.

_______   _______   6. The sinking of the Titanic was due to a series of foolish errors.

_______   _______   7. When disaster strikes, many people try to save items of no value.

_______   _______   8. Dreams reflect our feelings about others in our lives.

_______   _______   9. Family feuds can last for many generations.

_______   _______   10. In 1912, Americans were not as class conscious as the British.

_______   _______   11. It is acceptable to lie to save your life.

_______   _______   12. In historical fiction, the author may change historical facts to fit the story.

SOUNDER

by William Armstrong, HarperCollins, 1969

Put a check on the line under AGREE if you agree with the statement. Put a check on the line under DISAGREE if you disagree with the statement.

AGREE   DISAGREE

______   ______   1. Those who steal should receive harsh sentences, regardless of the reason for stealing.

______   ______   2. Neighbors who live far at can't help each other.

______   ______   3. Only a disturbed person is cruel to animals.

______   ______   4. The oldest child in a fatherless family should accept the responsibilities of a father.

______   ______   5. Anything stolen by a thief should be returned by a member of the thief's family.

______   ______   6. Learning to lose means accepting defeat with a smile.

______   ______   7. Some journeys have no end.

______   ______   8. A lonely boy and a kind teacher make a good combination.

______   ______   9. Education is the only way to escape poverty.

______   ______   10. A philosopher is a person with no common sense.

______   ______   11. One can be crippled in body but not in spirit.

______   ______   12. There is no hope of a decent life for one who cannot read.

STEPPING ON THE CRACKS

by Mary Downing Hahn, Houghton Mifflin, 1991

Put a check on the line under AGREE if you agree with the statement. Put a check on the line under DISAGREE if you disagree with the statement.

AGREE   DISAGREE

_______   _______   1. Getting even does not always bring satisfaction.

_______   _______   2. A bully is usually a very unhappy person.

_______   _______   3. Vandals never have a reason for destroying property.

_______   _______   4. Eavesdropping can only lead to trouble.

_______   _______   5. Children with no one to look after them are destined for a life of crime.

_______   _______   6. A scrupulously fair teacher is hard to find.

_______   _______   7. Sleeplessness is often caused by a troubled conscience.

_______   _______   8. A pacifist in time of war is a coward.

_______   _______   9. A person who mistreats an animal will also mistreat people.

_______   _______   10. A person who beats a child was probably beaten as a child.

_______   _______   11. Not being able to say goodbye to a friend is painful.

_______   _______   12. Telling a lie is sometimes necessary.

STONE FOX

by John Gardiner, HarperCollins, 1980

Put a check on the line under AGREE if you agree with the statement. Put a check on the line under DISAGREE if you disagree with the statement.

AGREE   DISAGREE

______   ______   1. Some folks just decide to stop living, and there is nothing you can do about it.

______   ______   2. A ten-year-old boy can run a farm all by himself.

______   ______   3. It is foolish to enter a race when all the odds are against you.

______   ______   4. Some problems are too overwhelming to be solved.

______   ______   5. A dog can be taught to pull a plow.

______   ______   6. It is true that where there s a will, there s a way.

______   ______   7. Determination is more important than knowledge in accomplishing a difficult task.

______   ______   8. It is natural to lose sleep the night before a big race.

______   ______   9. The greatest moment of tension in a race is three feet from the finish line.

______   ______   10. Some people would deliberately lose a race to allow another person to win.

______   ______   11. Wishing hard enough can make a wish come true.

______   ______   12. If yearly taxes are not paid, people may lose their homes.

STONEWORDS: A GHOST STORY

by Pam Conrad, HarperCollins, 1990

Put a check on the line under AGREE if you agree with the statement. Put a check on the line under DISAGREE if you disagree with the statement.

AGREE   DISAGREE

_____   _____   1. It is possible to have a friend that no one else can see.

_____   _____   2. An animal can often detect a presence that no one else is aware of.

_____   _____   3. Children are better off with a grandparent than with a mentally disturbed parent.

_____   _____   4. There is never any justification for vandalism.

_____   _____   5. If you wish for something hard enough, your wish will come true.

_____   _____   6. Ghosts are found only in stories.

_____   _____   7. It is impossible to change things that happened in the past.

_____   _____   8. You cannot force people to accept the truth if they are determined not to believe it.

_____   _____   9. Loneliness can make for strange companions.

_____   _____   10. The strongest force for good is love.

_____   _____   11. Growing up with grandparents is difficult because they do not understand children, who are of a different generation.

_____   _____   12. True friendship often involves sacrifice on the part of one of the friends.

A STRANGER AT GREEN KNOWE

by Lucy M. Boston, Harcourt, Brace, 1961

Put a check on the line under AGREE if you agree with the statement. Put a check on the line under DISAGREE if you disagree with the statement.

AGREE   DISAGREE

_____   _____   1. Wild animals should be captured for viewing by humans in zoos, otherwise many would never be seen.

_____   _____   2. There is no a good reason to kill a wild animal.

_____   _____   3. Wild animals in zoos often establish a bond with their keepers.

_____   _____   4. The greatest desire of an orphan is to be loved by a family.

_____   _____   5. An eleven-year-old would not enjoy spending time with an old person.

_____   _____   6. A gorilla that has escaped from a zoo is to be feared greatly.

_____   _____   7. Sometimes it is necessary to deceive those you love most.

_____   _____   8. Telling a lie to save an animal from captivity is not wrong.

_____   _____   9. It is better to die in freedom than to live a life in captivity.

_____   _____   10. A strong bond can be established between a human and a wild beast.

_____   _____   11. Cruelty toward animals should not be tolerated in any form.

_____   _____   12. Every living thing has a purpose on Earth; not one should be captured or destroyed.

STRAWBERRY GIRL
by *Lois Lenski,* Lippincott, 1945

Put a check on the line under AGREE if you agree with the statement. Put a check on the line under DISAGREE if you disagree with the statement.

AGREE   DISAGREE

_______   _______   1. No one wants to live on land too poor to produce crops.

_______   _______   2. It is possible without money to take an ugly place and make it beautiful.

_______   _______   3. Alcohol can make people do things they would not ordinarily do.

_______   _______   4. Change must begin with a positive attitude.

_______   _______   5. Sometimes it is necessary to hurt an animal.

_______   _______   6. If a neighbor destroys your property, you have a right to destroy the neighbor's property.

_______   _______   7. Some arguments can be settled only with force.

_______   _______   8. Poor people are unhappy most of the time.

_______   _______   9. Two wrongs don't make a right.

_______   _______   10. When you know there is trouble ahead, the best thing to do is hide.

_______   _______   11. Only cowards leave warning notes.

_______   _______   12. A fence that prevents animals from getting water should be torn down.

STRIDER

by Beverly Cleary, William Morrow, 1991

Put a check on the line under AGREE if you agree with the statement. Put a check on the line under DISAGREE if you disagree with the statement.

AGREE   DISAGREE

_____   _____   1. People who dump animals on country roads should be prosecuted.

_____   _____   2. Atment owners prefer people with no children.

_____   _____   3. Dog owners are responsible people.

_____   _____   4. When two boys share a dog, trouble lies ahead.

_____   _____   5. A trucker without a load is like a restaurant without food.

_____   _____   6. Wearing something that once belonged to a classmate is embarrassing.

_____   _____   7. Arguing with a teacher can lead to better grades.

_____   _____   8. If a teacher ridicules a student in class, the teacher obviously does not like children.

_____   _____   9. A grammatically correct composition is boring.

_____   _____   10. Apologizing is easier to do on the phone.

_____   _____   11. Having three good friends is better than having a lot of money.

_____   _____   12. It is impossible to teach a dog to read.

STUART LITTLE

by E. B. White, HarperCollins, 1973

Put a check on the line under AGREE if you agree with the statement. Put a check on the line under DISAGREE if you disagree with the statement.

AGREE   DISAGREE

_____   _____   1. Being a lot smaller than everyone else can be a handicap.

_____   _____   2. Showing off can lead to an injury.

_____   _____   3. Some people like to have mice in their houses.

_____   _____   4. A mouse and a bird may become good friends.

_____   _____   5. Little people can accomplish many tasks that larger people cannot.

_____   _____   6. Leaving home without telling anyone is inconsiderate.

_____   _____   7. When friends are in obvious danger, do not rush to help them.

_____   _____   8. A substitute teacher needs a sense of humor.

_____   _____   9. A falling barometer means fair weather.

_____   _____   10. Being chairman of the world would be an ideal job.

_____   _____   11. The best way to dispose of trash is to take it out in the countryside and dump it.

_____   _____   12. Making friends is not easy when you are different from everyone else.

SUMMER OF FEAR

by Lois Duncan, Little, Brown, 1976

Put a check on the line under AGREE if you agree with the statement. Put a check on the line under DISAGREE if you disagree with the statement.

AGREE   DISAGREE

______   ______   1. Sharing a room with a stranger can be difficult.

______   ______   2. A girl with haunted eyes harbors a lot of secrets.

______   ______   3. A usually peaceful dog gets its hackles up when it senses danger.

______   ______   4. A shopping spree can be fun, even if you have no money to spend.

______   ______   5. Friction between two people may cause discomfort for a third.

______   ______   6. A family should not have a pet if it has to be kept tied up.

______   ______   7. It is time to rebel when someone seems to be taking over your life.

______   ______   8. Some parents are more taken with strangers than with their own children.

______   ______   9. Trying to persuade someone to your point of view is easy if you have reasoned arguments.

______   ______   10. A successful impostor fools everyone.

______   ______   11. The love of family members for each other can overcome all troubles.

______   ______   12. Witches exist today.

SUMMER OF THE MONKEYS

by Wilson Rawls, Doubleday, 1976

Put a check on the line under AGREE if you agree with the statement. Put a check on the line under DISAGREE if you disagree with the statement.

AGREE   DISAGREE

_____   _____   1. Poor people who can't afford medical help have to live with their disabilities.

_____   _____   2. If you try something difficult and fail, people will laugh at you.

_____   _____   3. If you hear a loud cry in the woods, you should investigate.

_____   _____   4. Stepping on a large black snake in the woods can be fatal.

_____   _____   5. A monkey in the wild can outsmart a person.

_____   _____   6. Little sisters can be pests.

_____   _____   7. Never make an enemy of a goose.

_____   _____   8. If a dog fights a pack of monkeys, the monkeys will win.

_____   _____   9. Moonshiners work in secret, because making moonshine is against the law.

_____   _____   10. The best learning comes through experience.

_____   _____   11. There are things a young boy can't teach an old man.

_____   _____   12. There is music in the Ozark Mountains.

SUMMER OF THE SWANS

by Betsy Byars, Viking, 1970

Put a check on the line under AGREE if you agree with the statement. Put a check on the line under DISAGREE if you disagree with the statement.

AGREE   DISAGREE

_______   _______ 1. It is possible not to like yourself.

_______   _______ 2. Many people worry needlessly about what is wrong with them.

_______   _______ 3. Looking after a younger brother or sister can be a privilege.

_______   _______ 4. Accepting any kind of a dare is foolish.

_______   _______ 5. Beauty is in the eye of the beholder.

_______   _______ 6. One should take a premonition seriously.

_______   _______ 7. There are two sides to most stories.

_______   _______ 8. Pride is one reason for refusing help from a friend.

_______   _______ 9. People may surprise themselves by doing the impossible.

_______   _______ 10. Wishing hard enough can make a wish come true.

_______   _______ 11. Saying you are sorry is easy when you know you will be forgiven.

_______   _______ 12. Life is a series of huge, uneven steps.

SUSANNA OF THE ALAMO

by John Jakes, Harcourt Brace Jovanovich, 1986

Put a check on the line under AGREE if you agree with the statement. Put a check on the line under DISAGREE if you disagree with the statement.

AGREE   DISAGREE

_____   _____   1. Leaving a place where you have always lived is exciting.

_____   _____   2. Pioneer women did not need to know how to read or write.

_____   _____   3. Freedom is worth defending at any cost.

_____   _____   4. Living in a small space with many people can cause conflict.

_____   _____   5. When you know you cannot win an argument, the best thing to do is walk away.

_____   _____   6. Not reporting an injustice deserves a reward.

_____   _____   7. Strength can be shown in nonviolent ways.

_____   _____   8. It is foolish to fight when you know you cannot win.

_____   _____   9. Davy Crockett was a larger-than-life super hero.

_____   _____   10. Revenge can never be rewarding.

_____   _____   11. Powerful leaders on the same side often do not get along.

_____   _____   12. It is important to preserve historic buildings for future generations.

THE TALE OF DESPEREAUX: BEING THE STORY OF A MOUSE, A PRINCESS, SOME SOUP, AND A SPOOL OF THREAD

by Kate DiCamillo, Candlewick, 2003

Put a check on the line under AGREE if you agree with the statement. Put a check on the line under DISAGREE if you disagree with the statement.

AGREE   DISAGREE

______   ______   1. Many laws are unjust and should be repealed.

______   ______   2. No one would want to spend most of his or her days in a dungeon.

______   ______   3. People who refuse to conform are often ostracized.

______   ______   4. Mazes are built to trap people who can never find their way out.

______   ______   5. All of us trust many strangers every day.

______   ______   6. Unrequited love is a sad experience.

______   ______   7. Wishing for the impossible can make it happen.

______   ______   8. Some people make a mess of every job they undertake.

______   ______   9. Fear and courage often go together.

______   ______   10. It is better to tell a lie than to tell the truth and not be believed.

______   ______   11. It is better to be an only child than to have many brothers and sisters.

______   ______   12. Associating with others who are very different from you is asking for trouble.

TALES OF A FOURTH GRADE NOTHING

by *Judy Blume*, E. P. Dutton, 1972

Put a check on the line under AGREE if you agree with the statement. Put a check on the line under DISAGREE if you disagree with the statement.

AGREE   DISAGREE

———   ———   1. It would be great to win a turtle as a prize.

———   ———   2. Parents are not usually happy with new pets.

———   ———   3. Looking after a younger brother or sister can be a privilege.

———   ———   4. Coaxing a child to eat is wrong.

———   ———   5. Two-year-olds can often run a whole household.

———   ———   6. Accidents are most often caused by inattention.

———   ———   7. Little children receive more special treatment than their older brothers or sisters do.

———   ———   8. Some brothers and sisters never quarrel or fight.

———   ———   9. Three-year-olds should not be taken to a restaurant.

———   ———   10. When someone destroys your homework, you have a good excuse to give the teacher.

———   ———   11. A case of mistaken identity can lead to a fun adventure.

———   ———   12. Parents understand more than you think they do.

THE TALKING EARTH

by Jean Craighead George, HarperCollins, 1983

Put a check on the line under AGREE if you agree with the statement. Put a check on the line under DISAGREE if you disagree with the statement.

AGREE   DISAGREE

_____   _____   1. Leaving home for an indefinite period of time can be frightening.

_____   _____   2. "Curiosity killed the cat" is a proverb that should be heeded.

_____   _____   3. Only people with vivid imaginations see images in clouds.

_____   _____   4. You should never explore a cave alone.

_____   _____   5. It is impossible to gain the trust of a wild animal.

_____   _____   6. People today cannot live off the land as the early settlers did.

_____   _____   7. Sounds in a swamp are always frightening.

_____   _____   8. Old traditions should be cast aside in modern times.

_____   _____   9. The Earth talks to those who will listen.

_____   _____   10. Animals send many messages to humans.

_____   _____   11. A person may show prejudice against his or her own people.

_____   _____   12. The wisdom of old people is not relevant to life today.

A TASTE OF BLACKBERRIES

by Doris Buchanan Smith, Crowell, 1973

Put a check on the line under AGREE if you agree with the statement. Put a check on the line under DISAGREE if you disagree with the statement.

AGREE   DISAGREE

_____   _____   1. Nobody pays attention to a show-off.

_____   _____   2. It is not a good idea to accept a ride from a stranger.

_____   _____   3. It is hard to say no when a friend is in trouble.

_____   _____   4. Some people blame themselves for things that are not their fault.

_____   _____   5. If you are caught in a thunderstorm, stay away from trees.

_____   _____   6. A person who does not do his or her share of the work might have a good reason.

_____   _____   7. Shoving a stick down a beehole is not a good idea.

_____   _____   8. Your conscience may be bothersome even if you have done nothing wrong.

_____   _____   9. When eyes send a message, words are not needed.

_____   _____   10. A garden is a good place for thinking.

_____   _____   11. Answering a question with a question is one way to avoid conflict.

_____   _____   12. Sometimes you are your own worst enemy.

TIMOTHY OF THE CAY

by Theodore Taylor, Harcourt, Brace, 1993

Put a check on the line under AGREE if you agree with the statement. Put a check on the line under DISAGREE if you disagree with the statement.

AGREE   DISAGREE

______   ______   1. Guardian angels may exist in the form of humans.

______   ______   2. Being in the right place at the right time may save your life.

______   ______   3. Raising your hopes too high can only lead to disappointment.

______   ______   4. When what seemed to be a sure thing doesn't work out, give up.

______   ______   5. It is possible to feel like a stranger in your own home.

______   ______   6. Never do anything that doesn't make sense.

______   ______   7. Evil spirits exist, and it's possible to chase them away.

______   ______   8. Having a goal is essential to success.

______   ______   9. Some thoughts are hard to get rid of.

______   ______   10. There is more than one kind of courage.

______   ______   11. A prequel should follow a sequel.

______   ______   12. Wisdom seldom comes out of books.

TITANIC CROSSING

by Barbara Wiliams, Scholastic, 1995

Put a check on the line under AGREE if you agree with the statement. Put a check on the line under DISAGREE if you disagree with the statement.

AGREE   DISAGREE

______   ______   1. Life with a younger sister can be difficult.

______   ______   2. Some children are given heavy responsibilities early in life.

______   ______   3. A hypochondriac is never ill.

______   ______   4. A gift is more valuable if given by someone you admire.

______   ______   5. The best gift to receive is friendship.

______   ______   6. Any disaster is made worse when people panic.

______   ______   7. Foolish decisions are most likely made in a moment of crisis.

______   ______   8. Feelings may change drastically between the beginning and the end of a journey.

______   ______   9. It is possible to be fearful and brave at the same time.

______   ______   10. Grandparents and grandchildren do not understand each other, because they come from different generations.

______   ______   11. It is wrong for parents to choose a child s future career.

______   ______   12. On a sea voyage, third-class passengers have more fun than first-class passengers.

TOM'S MIDNIGHT GARDEN

by Philippa Pearce, Lippincott, 1959

Put a check on the line under AGREE if you agree with the statement. Put a check on the line under DISAGREE if you disagree with the statement.

AGREE   DISAGREE

_____   _____   1. Wishing for something hard enough will get you what you want.

_____   _____   2. Children with no friends to play with live in the world of the imagination.

_____   _____   3. It is not possible for a clock to strike 13.

_____   _____   4. People with insomnia are better off getting out of bed.

_____   _____   5. A place with garbage cans and a high fence can be transformed into a beautiful garden.

_____   _____   6. A strict, ill-tempered mother will have unhappy, lonely children.

_____   _____   7. It is possible for brothers to enjoy each other s company more than the company of friends.

_____   _____   8. One should never explore a strange new place alone.

_____   _____   9. Only a ghost can walk through walls and doors and leave no footprints.

_____   _____   10. When faced with supernatural events, it is best to say nothing.

_____   _____   11. Two people can wear the same pair of boots at the same time.

_____   _____   12. Saying goodbye to new friends can be as painful as saying goodbye to family.

TRACKER

by Gary Paulsen, Bradbury, 1984

Put a check on the line under AGREE if you agree with the statement. Put a check on the line under DISAGREE if you disagree with the statement.

AGREE   DISAGREE

______   ______   1. One should show every kindness to a critically ill person.

______   ______   2. Children raised on farms have more freedom than those raised in the city.

______   ______   3. A barn in the morning feels depressing because of the work that lies ahead.

______   ______   4. The only reason to track an animal is to kill it.

______   ______   5. Great joy and beauty are found in nature.

______   ______   6. Elderly people often display great knowledge.

______   ______   7. A swamp can provide a perfect cover for wounded animals.

______   ______   8. A threatened animal will nearly always attack.

______   ______   9. When your rifle sight is on a deer, shoot.

______   ______   10. Being tired beyond bearing leads to mistakes.

______   ______   11. A thing can be ugly and beautiful at the same time.

______   ______   12. Learning that death is a part of life is a hard but necessary lesson.

TRAPPED IN DEATH CAVE

by Bill Wallace, Holiday House, 1984

Put a check on the line under AGREE if you agree with the statement. Put a check on the line under DISAGREE if you disagree with the statement.

AGREE   DISAGREE

_____   _____   1. The best vacation would be in a cabin in the wild.

_____   _____   2. What appears at first to be an accident might actually not be an accident.

_____   _____   3. Stories are made up about people who are different by those who do not understand them.

_____   _____   4. A deserted, scary house may look to be in perfect condition.

_____   _____   5. Trespassing always means trouble.

_____   _____   6. When a friend calls you a chicken, never speak to that friend again.

_____   _____   7. The difference between courage and fear is action.

_____   _____   8. Only foolhardy people throw caution to the winds.

_____   _____   9. Exploring a cave alone is asking for trouble.

_____   _____   10. The old can be very helpful to the young.

_____   _____   11. American Indian cave drawings exist to leave warnings for the foolish.

_____   _____   12. Some problems have no solutions.

TRAPPED IN THE SLICKROCK CANYON

by Gloria Skurzynski, Lothrop, Lee & Shepard, 1984

Put a check on the line under AGREE if you agree with the statement. Put a check on the line under DISAGREE if you disagree with the statement.

AGREE   DISAGREE

_______   _______   1. There is never a valid reason for a parent to desert his or her family.

_______   _______   2. Adopting a superior attitude is one way to impress others.

_______   _______   3. Children of wealthy families are privileged and pampered.

_______   _______   4. Vandals who destroy natural beauty should be arrested and imprisoned.

_______   _______   5. Flash floods occur without warning and are extremely dangerous.

_______   _______   6. Quicksand appears only in adventure stories and does not really exist in nature.

_______   _______   7. The greater the cost of a pair of boots, the less likely they are to cause blisters.

_______   _______   8. No one can ever take the place of a best friend lost through death.

_______   _______   9. Artifacts are best kept in a museum to ensure their safety.

_______   _______   10. Nature can visit humans with severe hardships.

_______   _______   11. Excessive greed always leads to disaster.

_______   _______   12. Adversity may bring people together and help them to accept their differences.

TREASURE ISLAND

by Robert Louis Stevenson, Viking, 1992 (1883)

Put a check on the line under AGREE if you agree with the statement. Put a check on the line under DISAGREE if you disagree with the statement.

AGREE   DISAGREE

———   ———   1. An old seaman would have a face like leather.

———   ———   2. Owing money is not a problem if you can eventually pay it back.

———   ———   3. It is unwise to trust strangers, even if they are friends of a friend.

———   ———   4. As a group, sailors are superstitious people.

———   ———   5. When three people know a secret, soon everyone will know.

———   ———   6. Having something others want is not wrong.

———   ———   7. It is possible to travel in your mind and reach fascinating destinations.

———   ———   8. Hearing words not intended for your ears may get you into trouble.

———   ———   9. When friends begin to mistrust each other, a third party is usually responsible.

———   ———   10. When the odds in a fight are uneven, don't fight.

———   ———   11. Idle hands lead to mischief.

———   ———   12. Choosing between right and wrong is not always easy.

THE TRUE CONFESSIONS OF CHARLOTTE DOYLE

by Avi, Orchard Books, 1990

Put a check on the line under AGREE if you agree with the statement. Put a check on the line under DISAGREE if you disagree with the statement.

AGREE   DISAGREE

_____   _____   1. When sailors refuse to sign on to a ship, blame the captain.

_____   _____   2. The way to tell a liar from a truthful person is to look in his or her eyes.

_____   _____   3. If a captain is cruel and unreasonable, sailors have a right to mutiny.

_____   _____   4. Old people who try to give good advice should be ignored.

_____   _____   5. Ignorance of the law is a poor excuse.

_____   _____   6. A person can cause great harm without meaning to do so.

_____   _____   7. Always choose the easy way out of a difficult situation.

_____   _____   8. A female on a ship always brings bad luck.

_____   _____   9. It is easy to be forgiven if you say you are sorry.

_____   _____   10. Sometimes a cruel act can turn out to be a great kindness.

_____   _____   11. A sea voyage in 1832 would have been a pleasant experience.

_____   _____   12. People in responsible positions should always be trusted.

TUCK EVERLASTING

by Natalie Babbitt, Farrar, Straus & Giroux, 1975

Put a check on the line under AGREE if you agree with the statement. Put a check on the line under DISAGREE if you disagree with the statement.

AGREE   DISAGREE

———   ———   1. Land ownership can make one overly possessive.

———   ———   2. It is difficult to understand a person who does not want to be remembered by anyone.

———   ———   3. No one can look exactly the same for 87 years.

———   ———   4. Ignoring a problem is the best way to solve it, because it will solve itself.

———   ———   5. It is not wise to drink from a woodland stream.

———   ———   6. Some people never seem to grow any older.

———   ———   7. It is not wise to believe in fairy tales.

———   ———   8. Too much advice is worse than no advice at all.

———   ———   9. To live forever would be a desireable goal.

———   ———   10. Responsible people make a fortress out of duty.

———   ———   11. It is okay to tell a lie to keep someone out of trouble.

———   ———   12. When you want to help a friend but don't know what to do, go with your first idea.

THE TWENTY-ONE BALLOONS

by William Pene duBois, Viking, 1947

Put a check on the line under AGREE if you agree with the statement. Put a check on the line under DISAGREE if you disagree with the statement.

AGREE   DISAGREE

______   ______   1. The advantage of balloon travel is that you don't have far to fall.

______   ______   2. Starting a trip with no set destination can be exciting.

______   ______   3. A red-carpet welcome means that a person is being welcomed into prison.

______   ______   4. Owning many things can be a burden rather than a blessing.

______   ______   5. Having no work to do can be boring.

______   ______   6. It is okay to eat something if you don't know what it is, when others are eating it.

______   ______   7. Getting back on a horse means doing something you fear.

______   ______   8. It is possible to look into the crater of a volcano safely.

______   ______   9. Having material things means nothing if it is not accompanied by freedom.

______   ______   10. The most exciting carnival ride is the Ferris wheel.

______   ______   11. Living next to a live volcano is living dangerously.

______   ______   12. Exaggeration is at the heart of most good stories.

THE UNDERRUNNERS

by Margaret Mahy, Viking, 1992

Put a check on the line under AGREE if you agree with the statement. Put a check on the line under DISAGREE if you disagree with the statement.

AGREE   DISAGREE

_______   _______   1. A disorganized house equals a disorganized mind.

_______   _______   2. There is never any valid reason for a mother to desert her child.

_______   _______   3. A child with only one parent does not want to share that parent with another person.

_______   _______   4. Lonely children often dream up imaginary friends.

_______   _______   5. Every child wishes for a secret hideaway.

_______   _______   6. Children who have had bad experiences never give up hope of better days.

_______   _______   7. School bullies are insecure children who prey on others to prove their self-worth.

_______   _______   8. Sometimes, deceiving a parent is necessary.

_______   _______   9. Having one good friend is better than having many acquaintances.

_______   _______   10. Pretending to be someone else is never a good idea.

_______   _______   11. Life is like an underrunner, solid on top but with many hollows below.

_______   _______   12. Only the resourceful and independent can survive life's blows.

THE VIEW FROM SATURDAY

by *E. L. Konigsberg,* Atheneum, 1996

Put a check on the line under AGREE if you agree with the statement. Put a check on the line under DISAGREE if you disagree with the statement.

AGREE   DISAGREE

______   ______   1. Students would rather be on a sports team than on an academic team.

______   ______   2. Nitpicking is sometimes an excuse for jealousy.

______   ______   3. True friendship can survive long distances.

______   ______   4. One who is a watcher and a waiter misses the joys of life.

______   ______   5. Having a genius for an older brother makes one want to cause trouble just to get attention.

______   ______   6. Children can be cruel when they meet someone who is different.

______   ______   7. Guest lists are one way of being cruel to outsiders.

______   ______   8. When a tough choice has to be made, it is best to seek the advice of adults.

______   ______   9. One who will not risk making a mistake learns nothing new.

______   ______   10. Not being a team player can lead to the loss of the game.

______   ______   11. Malice never triumphs.

______   ______   12. Rules are made to be broken.

THE VIEW FROM THE CHERRY TREE

by Willow Davis Roberts, Macmillan, 1987

Put a check on the line under AGREE if you agree with the statement. Put a check on the line under DISAGREE if you disagree with the statement.

AGREE   DISAGREE

_____   _____   1. You can see the whole world go by if you watch from the top of a tree.

_____   _____   2. Some neighbors enjoy complaining and do it all the time.

_____   _____   3. A wedding in the family plays havoc with normal routines.

_____   _____   4. Some parents never listen to their children's concerns.

_____   _____   5. Borrowing money without letting the owner know is the same as stealing.

_____   _____   6. If someone wrongs you, get over it, don't try to get even.

_____   _____   7. Screams early in the morning probably come from a screech owl.

_____   _____   8. The best way to handle trouble is to run away from it.

_____   _____   9. The black sheep in a family marches to a different drummer.

_____   _____   10. When too many people are staying in a small house, tempers flare.

_____   _____   11. When reasoning with someone doesn't help, use force.

_____   _____   12. Drugs cause people to do strange things that they would not ordinarily do.

THE VILLAGE BY THE SEA

by Paula Fox, Orchard Books, 1988

Put a check on the line under AGREE if you agree with the statement. Put a check on the line under DISAGREE if you disagree with the statement.

AGREE   DISAGREE

_____   _____   1. The illness of a parent can change the life of the entire family.

_____   _____   2. Eccentric people are to be avoided, even though they appear to be gentle and wise.

_____   _____   3. Allowing yourself to be a bitter person is a form of self-pity.

_____   _____   4. Negative people should be avoided as they make life miserable for those around them.

_____   _____   5. Living with relatives you don't know can be a rewarding experience.

_____   _____   6. A good friend can make troubles seem easier to face.

_____   _____   7. A lot of people don't mind living in filthy houses.

_____   _____   8. In many families, the man does all the cooking and cleaning.

_____   _____   9. The most pleasant trip can be spoiled by a selfish person.

_____   _____   10. Vandals destroy property for no reason; they just enjoy doing it.

_____   _____   11. "Envy's a coal hissing hot from hell."

_____   _____   12. One should feel sorry for people who are filled with envy and hatred.

A WALK IN WOLF WOOD

by Mary Stewart, William Morrow, 1980

Put a check on the line under AGREE if you agree with the statement. Put a check on the line under DISAGREE if you disagree with the statement.

AGREE   DISAGREE

______   ______   1. A person crying in the forest is probably lost.

______   ______   2. Taking a walk alone in strange surroundings is not wise.

______   ______   3. Returning a lost item may be difficult.

______   ______   4. Parents are not always where they are supposed to be.

______   ______   5. Stealing someone's love is impossible.

______   ______   6. Werewolves exist only in stories.

______   ______   7. It is possible to dream when you are awake.

______   ______   8. There is such a thing as a false truth.

______   ______   9. Sometimes it is vital to pretend you are someone you are not.

______   ______   10. It is wrong to listen to someone else's conversation when he or she doesn't know you are there.

______   ______   11. It is permissible to tell a lie when helping someone in need.

______   ______   12. A medieval castle was a safe, comfortable place to live in.

WALK TWO MOONS

by Sharon Creech, HarperCollins, 1994

Put a check on the line under AGREE if you agree with the statement. Put a check on the line under DISAGREE if you disagree with the statement.

AGREE   DISAGREE

_______   _______   1. Moving to a town that is very different from the one you have left is an exciting adventure.

_______   _______   2. Not being able to predict what a person will do is frustrating.

_______   _______   3. Stay away from a person who seems to be followed by trouble.

_______   _______   4. Small acts of kindness are better than a large one-time gift.

_______   _______   5. A stranger who won't look you in the eye is probably shy.

_______   _______   6. Parents who play with their toddlers will listen to their teenagers.

_______   _______   7. Personal journals should never be read by others.

_______   _______   8. You should never accept a gift from someone you don't like.

_______   _______   9. Some people disappear on purpose, to upset their loved ones.

_______   _______   10. A dinner guest should never criticize the food.

_______   _______   11. If you visualize something happening, it will happen.

_______   _______   12. Sometimes it is important to walk in another's moccasins

WALKABOUT

by James Vance Marshall, William Morrow, 1971

Put a check on the line under AGREE if you agree with the statement. Put a check on the line under DISAGREE if you disagree with the statement.

AGREE   DISAGREE

_______   _______   1. "Civilized" is the opposite of "primitive."

_______   _______   2. Finding yourself in a completely unknown place is exciting.

_______   _______   3. Searching for food when you do not recognize plants can be fatal.

_______   _______   4. Laughter is a good antidote to fear.

_______   _______   5. It is possible to communicate clearly without words.

_______   _______   6. When a stranger takes over, it is difficult to trust him or her.

_______   _______   7. Life in a primitive society would be boring.

_______   _______   8. When cultures clash, war is inevitable.

_______   _______   9. The power of suggestion can work wonders.

_______   _______   10. A walkabout is a test of endurance.

_______   _______   11. Traveling on blind faith is a poor way to travel.

_______   _______   12. It is easy to misunderstand a look.

THE WAR WITH GRANDPA

by Robert Kimmel Smith, Delacorte, 1985

Put a check on the line under AGREE if you agree with the statement. Put a check on the line under DISAGREE if you disagree with the statement.

AGREE   DISAGREE

_____   _____   1. You can never win an argument with a parent.

_____   _____   2. Children have no rights in their own homes.

_____   _____   3. When you have to do something you don't want to do, do it immediately, don't put it off.

_____   _____   4. A depressed person could be cheerful if he or she wanted to.

_____   _____   5. Guerrilla warfare means all-out war with no holds barred.

_____   _____   6. It takes two sides to create a disagreement.

_____   _____   7. The best ideas come when you are asleep.

_____   _____   8. A good way to end an argument is to accept the other person s point of view.

_____   _____   9. The advice of friends should always be ignored.

_____   _____   10. Waiting for the other shoe to drop is scary.

_____   _____   11. It is never too late to apologize.

_____   _____   12. When three generations share a home, there is bound to be conflict.

THE WATSONS GO TO BIRMINGHAM

by Christopher Paul Curtis, Delacorte, 1995

Put a check on the line under AGREE if you agree with the statement. Put a check on the line under DISAGREE if you disagree with the statement.

AGREE   DISAGREE

_______   _______ 1. When your older brother is the school hero, the only way for you to attract attention is to be a troublemaker.

_______   _______ 2. Usually the smartest kid in the class has few friends.

_______   _______ 3. If you are tricked out of something you value, find a way to get even.

_______   _______ 4. It is cruel to tease people because of their ragged clothes.

_______   _______ 5. When the school bully heads your way, run!

_______   _______ 6. Parents who give harsh punishments were themselves punished harshly when they were children.

_______   _______ 7. Changing one's image is impossible.

_______   _______ 8. Children can't help being prejudiced; they learned the prejudice from their parents.

_______   _______ 9. A person with a sassy laugh is asking for trouble.

_______   _______ 10. Many teens deliberately dress to provoke their parents.

_______   _______ 11. Blind prejudice is no reason for acts of violence.

_______   _______ 12. A small size and a large measure of respect may go together.

THE WAVE

by Margaret Hodges, Houghton Mifflin, 1957

Put a check on the line under AGREE if you agree with the statement. Put a check on the line under DISAGREE if you disagree with the statement.

AGREE   DISAGREE

______   ______   1. Japan is the only country that has experienced tidal waves.

______   ______   2. A grandson should treat his grandfather with great respect.

______   ______   3. Villagers may go to see a wise old man if they have problems.

______   ______   4. Earthquake weather feels the same as normal weather.

______   ______   5. An earthquake will not frighten a child who has never experienced one.

______   ______   6. Nature can both give and take away.

______   ______   7. It is foolish to sacrifice time or money for people you don't know.

______   ______   8. If villagers saw rice fields on fire, they would run to help put the fires out.

______   ______   9. An old man watching his property burn would feel despair.

______   ______   10. A tidal wave can wipe out an entire village.

______   ______   11. A rich man who loses his wealth becomes bitter.

______   ______   12. No one can predict when a tidal wave might strike.

WEASEL

by Cynthia DeFelice, Macmillan, 1990

Put a check on the line under AGREE if you agree with the statement. Put a check on the line under DISAGREE if you disagree with the statement.

AGREE   DISAGREE

_______   _______   1. Isolation and hard work were integral parts of every pioneer family's life.

_______   _______   2. Pioneer children were often left alone out of necessity.

_______   _______   3. Following a stranger is not wise, even if it might mean saving a life.

_______   _______   4. Some pioneer men killed both men and beasts just for the pleasure of killing.

_______   _______   5. If a person accepts responsibility for an animal, the animal's welfare comes first.

_______   _______   6. Saving your own skin is more important than seeking revenge.

_______   _______   7. A person can be keeping an eye on you without your knowing it.

_______   _______   8. Any kindness should be repaid as quickly as possible.

_______   _______   9. It is wrong to kill a helpless man, even if he is a bloodthirsty murderer.

_______   _______   10. One does not have to become a savage to live in a savage land.

_______   _______   11. The only thing certain about life is change. Nothing ever stays the same.

_______   _______   12. Daniel Boone always treated American Indian tribes fairly.

A WEEK IN THE WOODS

by Andrew Clements, Simon & Schuster, 2002

Put a check on the line under AGREE if you agree with the statement. Put a check on the line under DISAGREE if you disagree with the statement.

AGREE   DISAGREE

______   ______   1. City kids who move to a small town are usually labeled stuck-up and lazy.

______   ______   2. Some people refuse to adjust to a new lifestyle and become permanently angry.

______   ______   3. Being away from parents for a long time results in an unhappy child who is likely to get into trouble.

______   ______   4. Using the Internet for shopping is not usually the wisest thing to do.

______   ______   5. The best way to attract an adult's attention is to do something upsetting.

______   ______   6. You should never take the blame for another's actions even if that person is a good friend.

______   ______   7. When your troubles seem too large, the best thing to do is run away.

______   ______   8. A child who refuses to take part in school activities has low self-esteem and needs to be shown how to succeed.

______   ______   9. It is often too late to change your attitude if people have formed a firm opinion of you.

______   ______   10. Remorse is a feeling that emerges when you have harmed someone else.

______   ______   11. The best way to right a wrong is to say you're sorry.

______   ______   12. Good things can often result from a bad situation.

THE WEIRDO

by Theodore Taylor, Harcourt Brace Jovanovich, 1991

Put a check on the line under AGREE if you agree with the statement. Put a check on the line under DISAGREE if you disagree with the statement.

AGREE   DISAGREE

_____   _____   1. A badly disfigured person might retreat from society.

_____   _____   2. Environmentalists and hunters don't get along.

_____   _____   3. It is necessary to track the bear population in a wildlife refuge.

_____   _____   4. Hunters can always hunt on their own property.

_____   _____   5. A family that has trouble communicating should seek outside help.

_____   _____   6. When an environment changes, the wildlife will suffer.

_____   _____   7. You should think twice before championing an unpopular cause.

_____   _____   8. Heated opposition is not the same as dissent.

_____   _____   9. No cause is worth your life.

_____   _____   10. The only thing certain in life is change.

_____   _____   11. Hiding from the world is counterproductive.

_____   _____   12. Harvesting bears means killing them to reduce the bear population in a confined area.

THE WESTING GAME

by Ellen Raskin, E. P. Dutton, 1978

Put a check on the line under AGREE if you agree with the statement. Put a check on the line under DISAGREE if you disagree with the statement.

AGREE   DISAGREE

_______   _______ 1. Getting a luxury apartment at a very low price may turn out to be a disappointment.

_______   _______ 2. Spending one hour in a haunted house would be thrilling.

_______   _______ 3. The best way to get people into a restaurant is to dare them to try the food.

_______   _______ 4. A person who is never noticed wants not to be noticed.

_______   _______ 5. Finding you are an heir means you will receive lots of money.

_______   _______ 6. Relatives are always entitled to an inheritance when someone passes on.

_______   _______ 7. When playing a game with a large reward for the winner, some players will cheat.

_______   _______ 8. Clues that don't make sense are best ignored.

_______   _______ 9. It is sometimes necessary to give up a dream.

_______   _______ 10. In any group of people, differences of opinion are to be expected.

_______   _______ 11. Playing the stock market can be risky unless you are a stockbroker.

_______   _______ 12. A clear conscience is worth a million dollars.

WESTMARK

by Lloyd Alexander, E. P. Dutton, 1981

Put a check on the line under AGREE if you agree with the statement. Put a check on the line under DISAGREE if you disagree with the statement.

AGREE   DISAGREE

______   ______   1. A kingdom's power held in the hands of one person may be a disaster.

______   ______   2. Freedom of the press equals freedom of the people.

______   ______   3. A charlatan is one who lives by fooling others.

______   ______   4. A child cannot survive without the protection of a family.

______   ______   5. Nightmares are the result of real-life fears.

______   ______   6. A spiritualist can communicate with the dead.

______   ______   7. Disobeying parents may lead to disaster.

______   ______   8. People suffer from amnesia only in books and plays.

______   ______   9. There is never a valid reason to take a human life.

______   ______   10. A wise leader is in constant touch with those he or she leads.

______   ______   11. Courage may take many different forms.

______   ______   12. Living in a democracy is far better than living under the rule of a kind, wise monarch.

WHEN HITLER STOLE THE PINK RABBIT

by Judith Kerr, Coward-McCann, 1972

Put a check on the line under AGREE if you agree with the statement. Put a check on the line under DISAGREE if you disagree with the statement.

AGREE   DISAGREE

_____   _____   1. Many Jewish families were able to leave Germany before Hitler gained power.

_____   _____   2. One who is highly respected as a writer in one country may be unknown in another country.

_____   _____   3. In any war, one side is always right and the other wrong.

_____   _____   4. It is possible to be an honor student in one school yet fail in another school.

_____   _____   5. Learning a new language is easier for children than for adults.

_____   _____   6. No problem is too difficult if a family stays together.

_____   _____   7. Throughout the ages, many people have been persecuted for their beliefs.

_____   _____   8. A father may have a very good reason to leave his family.

_____   _____   9. The most difficult part of living in a strange country is not knowing the language.

_____   _____   10. Any government can take away all the possessions of a family without compensation.

_____   _____   11. Millions of Jews who did not escape Hitler's Germany were murdered.

_____   _____   12. Many refugees leave a comfortable living for a life of poverty.

WHEN ZACHARY BEAVER CAME TO TOWN

by Kimberly Willis Holt, Dell Yearling, 1999

Put a check on the line under AGREE if you agree with the statement. Put a check on the line under DISAGREE if you disagree with the statement.

AGREE   DISAGREE

_____   _____   1. It is unwise to judge a person by appearance only.

_____   _____   2. Things that seem crazy to some people make perfect sense to others.

_____   _____   3. Losing a contest may be a very good thing.

_____   _____   4. A circus would be a big event in a small town.

_____   _____   5. To be an outcast is not a bad thing.

_____   _____   6. Looking after a little sister can be a joy.

_____   _____   7. To make it big in show business, you need determination more than talent.

_____   _____   8. When a child is left alone, disaster may follow.

_____   _____   9. No one wants to listen to classical music today.

_____   _____   10. Having a lifelong wish fulfilled is not always a good thing.

_____   _____   11. When you see someone doing wrong, tell those in authority.

_____   _____   12. The best way to right a wrong is to say you are sorry.

WHERE THE LILIES BLOOM

by Bill and Vera Cleaver, Lippincott, 1969

Put a check on the line under AGREE if you agree with the statement. Put a check on the line under DISAGREE if you disagree with the statement.

AGREE   DISAGREE

______   ______   1. Life in the Appalachian Mountains is hard on most people.

______   ______   2. Neighbors may be good or bad, depending on their income.

______   ______   3. Think carefully and read every word before signing a contract.

______   ______   4. Freedom means different things to different people.

______   ______   5. It is impossible to farm rocky soil.

______   ______   6. Poor people don't appreciate charity or pity.

______   ______   7. Some terrible secrets must be kept within the family.

______   ______   8. Posting a warning about wild animals is a good way to keep visitors away.

______   ______   9. It is impossible to survive the winter in a badly damaged house.

______   ______   10. A promise made to a dying person does not need to be kept.

______   ______   11. A family of four can support itself by wildcrafting.

______   ______   12. There are good reasons to keep farm animals in the house.

WHERE THE RED FERN GROWS

by Wilson Rawls, Doubleday, 1961

Put a check on the line under AGREE if you agree with the statement. Put a check on the line under DISAGREE if you disagree with the statement.

AGREE   DISAGREE

———   ———   1. Good memories are worth more than gold.

———   ———   2. Going to school at home would be fun.

———   ———   3. A person who won't break a promise is stubborn.

———   ———   4. It is dangerous for a dog in the woods to meet a wild animal.

———   ———   5. Country people have a poorer education than city people.

———   ———   6. City people are smarter than country people.

———   ———   7. A bully is someone who dislikes himself.

———   ———   8. Some superstitions should be believed, since they come from human experience.

———   ———   9. If two dogs fight a mountain lion, they will lose.

———   ———   10. Some boys get along better with their grandfathers than with their fathers.

———   ———   11. It's bad luck for a rabbit to cross your path from left to right.

———   ———   12. Hearing a screech owl means a sickness is coming.

THE WHIPPING BOY

by Sid Fleischman, Greenwillow Books, 1986

Put a check on the line under AGREE if you agree with the statement. Put a check on the line under DISAGREE if you disagree with the statement.

AGREE   DISAGREE

_____   _____   1. A child who plays a prank on dinner guests should be punished.

_____   _____   2. The job of a tutor is to teach a child to play an instrument.

_____   _____   3. Not having enough to eat is one reason why a child might run away from home.

_____   _____   4. Being lost in the woods on a foggy night would be exciting.

_____   _____   5. Letting someone believe a lie is not always wrong.

_____   _____   6. Starving people will eat food that is spoiled or rotten.

_____   _____   7. It is unfair to be punished for another's misdeeds.

_____   _____   8. Revealing a secret can sometimes cause joy.

_____   _____   9. One should help a friend in need, even if there is danger involved.

_____   _____   10. There is no pleasure in seeing others punished.

_____   _____   11. Careful people leap before they look.

_____   _____   12. Life in a palace would be better than life in the sewers.

WHO KNEW THERE'D BE GHOSTS?

by Bill Brittain, HarperCollins, 1985

Put a check on the line under AGREE if you agree with the statement. Put a check on the line under DISAGREE if you disagree with the statement.

AGREE   DISAGREE

_______   _______   1. Laughing at someone's size is okay if the other person laughs with you.

_______   _______   2. Exploring an abandoned mansion is foolish.

_______   _______   3. The best games to play require the use of imagination.

_______   _______   4. A talking head minus a body could appear only in a book.

_______   _______   5. It takes a lot of courage to stand up to adults.

_______   _______   6. A practical parent has no imagination.

_______   _______   7. When good friends don't believe you, drop them as friends.

_______   _______   8. One vote may be extremely important.

_______   _______   9. The truest test of friendship is trust.

_______   _______   10. Progress in a town is not always a positive thing.

_______   _______   11. Children can't do anything to change city laws.

_______   _______   12. A house that is real, living history should never be torn down.

WHO REALLY KILLED COCK ROBIN?

by Jean Craighead George, E. P. Dutton, 1971

Put a check on the line under AGREE if you agree with the statement. Put a check on the line under DISAGREE if you disagree with the statement.

AGREE   DISAGREE

———   ———   1. Many wild birds die from natural causes.

———   ———   2. Much can be learned by keeping a journal about the habits of a wild animal.

———   ———   3. People pollute the Earth many times each day.

———   ———   4. When people in authority don't listen, yell more loudly.

———   ———   5. One reason to steal a dead bird is to stuff it and mount it on a wall.

———   ———   6. Children don't need to be concerned about the environment.

———   ———   7. Convincing a crowd of people to change their minds is impossible.

———   ———   8. One should never be accused of wrong doing without solid evidence.

———   ———   9. Avoid any wild animal that appears friendly.

———   ———   10. Factories are the worst polluters of the environment.

———   ———   11. It is possible to feel guilt for another's actions.

———   ———   12. Government agencies often issue orders without concern for those who must carry them out.

WHO WAS THAT MASKED MAN, ANYWAY?

by Avi, Orchard Books, 1992

Put a check on the line under AGREE if you agree with the statement. Put a check on the line under DISAGREE if you disagree with the statement.

AGREE   DISAGREE

_____   _____   1. A radio adventure broadcast in 1945 would not be interesting today.

_____   _____   2. Ignoring an "off limits" sign may lead to a jail sentence.

_____   _____   3. Living in the world of the imagination has no practical value.

_____   _____   4. A serious talk with your teacher is to be avoided.

_____   _____   5. Having a war hero in the family means ignoring the contributions of others.

_____   _____   6. Communication between parents and children can be difficult.

_____   _____   7. Matchmaking should be avoided; it can often backfire.

_____   _____   8. The best way to deal with a serious situation is to pretend it does not exist.

_____   _____   9. Having a one-track mind is the best way to solve a problem.

_____   _____   10. Intelligent people don't need to ask questions.

_____   _____   11. Some people are totally insensitive to the feelings of others.

_____   _____   12. One way to escape the real world is to live in a dream world.

THE WIDE WINDOW

by Lemony Snicket, HarperCollins, 2000

Put a check on the line under AGREE if you agree with the statement. Put a check on the line under DISAGREE if you disagree with the statement.

AGREE   DISAGREE

_____   _____   1. No one wants to live with a relative he or she hasn't met.

_____   _____   2. People with irrational fears should seek medical help.

_____   _____   3. People are judged first by the way they speak.

_____   _____   4. When someone appears in disguise, it must be Halloween.

_____   _____   5. No one would have a huge library filled only with books about grammar.

_____   _____   6. A proper business card proves who you are.

_____   _____   7. You never know what to expect from a person who resembles a chameleon.

_____   _____   8. Some people make themselves ill on purpose, to get attention.

_____   _____   9. When a situation seems hopeless, give up.

_____   _____   10. Cold meals are as good for you as hot meals.

_____   _____   11. A house built on stilts over a lake would be a dangerous place to live.

_____   _____   12. Never take a boat out on a lake when storm clouds are overhead.

WILD MAN ISLAND

by Will Hobbs, HarperCollins, 2002

Put a check on the line under AGREE if you agree with the statement. Put a check on the line under DISAGREE if you disagree with the statement.

AGREE   DISAGREE

_____   _____   1. Not staying with a group on a camping trip may get you into trouble.

_____   _____   2. Taking risky chances is the thing to do if the reward is big enough.

_____   _____   3. It is impossible to survive alone on an island without food and water for more than four days.

_____   _____   4. Slugs and bugs would taste good if you were hungry enough.

_____   _____   5. Never trust a stranger, even if you desperately need help.

_____   _____   6. You can learn a lot from people you don't know.

_____   _____   7. Never let someone trust you with a secret. If someone else reveals it, you could be blamed.

_____   _____   8. Home is never the same after you have been away for a long time.

_____   _____   9. After trying and failing many times, it is best to give up.

_____   _____   10. Helping out a friend is more rewarding for you than for the friend.

_____   _____   11. Any task is possible as long as you believe you can do it.

_____   _____   12. Animals have a strong sense of direction. If you are lost, follow an animal.

WISHES, KISSES, AND PIGS

by Betsy Hearne, Margaret K. McElderry Books, 2001

Put a check on the line under AGREE if you agree with the statement. Put a check on the line under DISAGREE if you disagree with the statement.

AGREE   DISAGREE

_____   _____   1. Little brothers can be a big pain and should be made to disappear.

_____   _____   2. Messing with magic you don't understand can get you into big trouble.

_____   _____   3. Be careful what you wish for; you may receive it.

_____   _____   4. It is impossible to undo the results of a wish.

_____   _____   5. Wishing on a star will make the wish come true.

_____   _____   6. A talking pig could appear only in a fantasy tale.

_____   _____   7. It is possible to put someone in a trance-like state if you know how to do it.

_____   _____   8. If you are unjustly accused of stealing, you should commit a real crime, since everyone believes you are a criminal.

_____   _____   9. A father would not leave his family without a very good reason for doing so.

_____   _____   10. Magic is for entertainment only; there is no real magic.

_____   _____   11. Music will soothe restless animals.

_____   _____   12. Not everything can be fixed with magic.

THE WITCH OF BLACKBIRD POND

by Elizabeth George Speare, Dell, 1958

Put a check on the line under AGREE if you agree with the statement. Put a check on the line under DISAGREE if you disagree with the statement.

AGREE   DISAGREE

______   ______   1. When diverse cultures, meet there is bound to be trouble.

______   ______   2. Traveling a long distance by sea can be exhausting and exciting at the same time.

______   ______   3. A lively young girl will never learn to fit into a stern household.

______   ______   4. To show loyalty to a government, one should not criticize it.

______   ______   5. Always stand up to someone who is not being fair.

______   ______   6. Ignorance and prejudice go hand in hand.

______   ______   7. Well-meaning people often cause trouble.

______   ______   8. Behavior that is accepted in one culture may seem shocking in another.

______   ______   9. Hard work is good for the body and the mind.

______   ______   10. Only ignorant people would accuse someone of witchcraft.

______   ______   11. To find happiness in a new world, you must adopt its customs.

______   ______   12. It is difficult to find a friend when you really need one.

THE WITCHES

by Roald Dahl, Jonathan Cape, 1983

Put a check on the line under AGREE if you agree with the statement. Put a check on the line under DISAGREE if you disagree with the statement.

AGREE   DISAGREE

_______   _______   1. A trip with a grandmother can be an exciting trip.

_______   _______   2. An automobile may turn into a monster when driven by a teen.

_______   _______   3. Playing tricks can be fun, especially when you do not know how the person being tricked will react.

_______   _______   4. Grandmothers' stories are almost always boring.

_______   _______   5. Pretending to be someone else may lead to trouble.

_______   _______   6. No one would want to have the power to turn another person into stone.

_______   _______   7. No one would want a gift of two white mice.

_______   _______   8. Mice can be trained to be tightrope walkers.

_______   _______   9. Missing toes on both feet would give you a crooked walk.

_______   _______   10. People who never take baths have low self-esteem.

_______   _______   11. There are many advantages to being small enough to fit into a purse.

_______   _______   12. Being zapped into a frog by a witch could happen only in a fantasy tale.

THE WIZARD OF OZ

by L. Frank Baum, World Publishing, 1972 (1900)

Put a check on the line under AGREE if you agree with the statement. Put a check on the line under DISAGREE if you disagree with the statement.

AGREE   DISAGREE

______   ______   1. Cyclones are more deadly than hurricanes.

______   ______   2. Waking up in a strange place can be exciting.

______   ______   3. Beware of strangers who offer hospitality.

______   ______   4. In the wrong hands, a match can cause trouble.

______   ______   5. Forests are essential to human survival.

______   ______   6. More laws are needed to protect wildlife.

______   ______   7. Never begin a journey if you don't know where it will end.

______   ______   8. Fear and courage are often found together in the same person.

______   ______   9. Most people have their hearts desire and don't know it.

______   ______   10. Wild plants are as dangerous as wild animals.

______   ______   11. Many hands make a task much lighter.

______   ______   12. "Nothing is given for nothing." There is a price to pay for everything we receive.

WOLF RIDER

by Avi, Macmillan, 1986

Put a check on the line under AGREE if you agree with the statement. Put a check on the line under DISAGREE if you disagree with the statement.

AGREE   DISAGREE

————   ————   1. A phone call from a stranger should be ignored.

————   ————   2. One way to remember a conversation is to visualize it in your mind.

————   ————   3. Mixed feelings lead to no decision being made at all.

————   ————   4. You should leave a gathering if you feel out of place there.

————   ————   5. It is impossible to get rid of a nagging thought.

————   ————   6. It is not possible to read another's thoughts.

————   ————   7. A plan is more important than courage in taking command of a situation.

————   ————   8. Friendships are dissolved when motives are misunderstood.

————   ————   9. When a person is obsessed with a notion, others may suffer.

————   ————   10. Pretending nothing is wrong is the same as running away from a problem.

————   ————   11. The best way to gain power over a person is to use force.

————   ————   12. The urge to speak out is overwhelming when you know you are right.

THE WOLVES OF WILLOUGHBY CHASE

by Joan Aiken, Doubleday, 2004 (1962)

Put a check on the line under AGREE if you agree with the statement. Put a check on the line under DISAGREE if you disagree with the statement.

AGREE   DISAGREE

_____   _____   1. Living in an English manor house would be fun.

_____   _____   2. Controlling your temper is difficult when you are unjustly accused.

_____   _____   3. A wolf can be dangerous when it travels alone.

_____   _____   4. Good fortune is often tinged with guilt.

_____   _____   5. Disregarding a warning may lead to an exciting adventure.

_____   _____   6. It is possible to be a prisoner in your own home.

_____   _____   7. Lively behavior is often mistaken for disrespect.

_____   _____   8. Following rules, even when they are unjust, is wise.

_____   _____   9. It was impossible to cure pneumonia before antibiotics were introduced.

_____   _____   10. It is impossible for a child to convince an adult of another adult's guilt.

_____   _____   11. Justice is its own reward.

_____   _____   12. In the nineteenth century, trains provided most of the opportunities for long-distance travel.

A WRINKLE IN TIME

by *Madeline L. Engle*, Farrar, Straus & Giroux, 1962

Put a check on the line under AGREE if you agree with the statement. Put a check on the line under DISAGREE if you disagree with the statement.

AGREE   DISAGREE

______   ______   1. Cruel, insensitive people make fun of those who are different.

______   ______   2. Popular people may be lonely.

______   ______   3. There may be life on other planets.

______   ______   4. A little brother needs to fight his own battles, even if challenged by someone bigger.

______   ______   5. The concept of a wrinkle in time and space is fantasy.

______   ______   6. A person reported missing may have chosen to disappear.

______   ______   7. The struggle between good and evil will always be with us.

______   ______   8. To be human is to have faults.

______   ______   9. People cherish the familiar because they are afraid of change.

______   ______   10. Individuality means doing what you want whenever you want.

______   ______   11. A single citizen can effect change in a society.

______   ______   12. The greatest power a human being can have is love.

YANG THE YOUNGEST AND HIS TERRIBLE EAR

by Lensky Namioka, Little, Brown, 1992

Put a check on the line under AGREE if you agree with the statement. Put a check on the line under DISAGREE if you disagree with the statement.

AGREE   DISAGREE

_______   _______   1. Not being musical in a musical family is a handicap.

_______   _______   2. Being tone deaf means you do not hear the music other people hear.

_______   _______   3. Wanting to please but not being able to please is a terrible burden.

_______   _______   4. When starting a new school, you will always have problems with other students.

_______   _______   5. When a bully takes something of yours, tell the teacher.

_______   _______   6. Every person is able to do something well.

_______   _______   7. Everyone has felt left out at one time or another.

_______   _______   8. Opposites nearly always complement each other.

_______   _______   9. No child would deliberately displease a parent.

_______   _______   10. Expecting a disaster is a sure way to make one occur.

_______   _______   11. At times it is acceptable to pretend to be something you are not.

_______   _______   12. Accepting the inevitable means giving up.

YOLANDA'S GENIUS

by Carol Fenner, Simon & Schuster, 1996

Put a check on the line under AGREE if you agree with the statement. Put a check on the line under DISAGREE if you disagree with the statement.

AGREE   DISAGREE

_____   _____   1. Moving from a large city to a small town requires a big adjustment.

_____   _____   2. One can be extremely talented in music while showing little talent for academic learning.

_____   _____   3. Teachers will never recognize genius in a child who has difficulty learning to read.

_____   _____   4. Determination can overcome most obstacles.

_____   _____   5. Children who have difficulty learning in first grade will have difficulty learning in all the grades to come.

_____   _____   6. The best way to attract attention in school is to be a behavior problem.

_____   _____   7. It would be hard not to feel awkward if you were the new kid in town.

_____   _____   8. People who live in big cities are generally scornful of small towns.

_____   _____   9. Physically tough people are usually bullies.

_____   _____   10. No one wants to be friends with the smartest kid in the class.

_____   _____   11. Parents usually see in their children only what they want to see.

_____   _____   12. It is impossible to convince people of the truth if they are determined not to believe it.

YOUR MOVE, J. P.

by Lois Lowry, Houghton Mifflin, 1990

Put a check on the line under AGREE if you agree with the statement. Put a check on the line under DISAGREE if you disagree with the statement.

AGREE   DISAGREE

_______   _______   1. Falling in love is painful.

_______   _______   2. Inventors are never satisfied with the way things are.

_______   _______   3. Promises made in a hurry are difficult to keep.

_______   _______   4. People exaggerate the truth to impress others.

_______   _______   5. Some people prefer to experience ill health.

_______   _______   6. Many times it is better to be an observer than a participant.

_______   _______   7. Getting caught in a lie is a good thing; it allows the truth to surface.

_______   _______   8. A fad and a trend are not the same thing.

_______   _______   9. There is no satisfaction in being admired for something you don't deserve.

_______   _______   10. The more you know about someone, the better you like that person.

_______   _______   11. Telling lies can be a bad habit to break.

_______   _______   12. The best way to get someone to notice you is to do a good deed.

Z FOR ZACHARIAH

by Robert C. O'Brien, Atheneum, 1975

Put a check on the line under AGREE if you agree with the statement. Put a check on the line under DISAGREE if you disagree with the statement.

AGREE   DISAGREE

______   ______   1. Being the only person left in the world would be devastating.

______   ______   2. Every human being needs someone to talk to.

______   ______   3. A warning deliberately given too late is not a warning at all.

______   ______   4. An evening s entertainment is not possible without electricity.

______   ______   5. "Necessity is the mother of invention" is a foolish saying.

______   ______   6. Compromise is not always easy but often necessary.

______   ______   7. Learning to walk all over again is harder than learning the first time.

______   ______   8. If someone tries to control you, the best thing to do is run away.

______   ______   9. Some people never show gratitude for the help they receive from others.

______   ______   10. There would be no survivors in a nuclear war.

______   ______   11. One way to calm feelings of distress is to sing.

______   ______   12. When two people want the same thing, the physically stronger always wins.

INDEX

About the Author

NANCY POLETTE is an educator with over 30 years experience. She has authored over 150 professional books. She lives and works in Missouri where she is Professor at Lindenwood College.